SELKIE SUMMER

SELKIE SUMMER

Ken MacLeod

NewCon Press
England

First published in the UK, May 2020 by
NewCon Press
41 Wheatsheaf Road,
Alconbury Weston,
Cambs, PE28 4LF

NCP237 (limited edition hardback)
NCP238 (paperback)

10 9 8 7 6 5 4 3 2 1

ISBN:

978-1-912950-63-1 (hardback)
978-1-912950-63-8 (paperback)

Cover art by Ben Baldwin
Cover layout by Ian Whates

Typesetting and minor editorial meddling by Ian Whates
Book layout by Ian Whates

Certain Scotch divines, not all of the *fanatical* persuasion, have instanc'd the *selkie*, as a visible proof of devils, angels, and the like phantoms (as we would perforce have to call such, for our lack of experience of the same, were it not for the testimony of *Scripture*). But 'tis plain to any man of sense, that the selkie is of a species with what the Greeks call'd *dryads*, the Mahometans *djinni*, the Negroes (as I've heard, by report of a ship's captain in Leith) *juju*, the Irish the *sidh*, *&c.*

In all such cases, 'twere but sophistical to consider so manifestly material a being (albeit of matter more subtle than the common sort) a *visible spirit*. The grossness of their appetites, and the wantonness of their actions, are further evidence of their embodiment. Morever, none of these beings are reckoned, even by the clergy of the prevalent religion, of those times and places, to be of a similar nature to their imagin'd gods, spirits, or (in the case of the Papists) saints. Quite the contrary.

How ridiculous, therefore, must it appear, when so much is understood by the meanest intellects, under the sway of *heathen* or popish superstition, for men of learning to drag the selkie, as 'twere by the *hair*, into evidence for the truth of the natural, or even of the *revealed*, religion?

'Tis true, the ability of the selkie (and I dare say the others, though exact testimony is wanting) to vary his *shape*, may well be marvelled at; but is it more marvellous, or less natural, than that of the *chameleon* to change his colour?

David Hume, 'Of beings rational, other than Man', an unpublished fragment from the MS of *The Natural History of Religion*, Edinburgh, 1777.

One

For no reason I could see, the bus stopped. I peered through the steamed-up, rain-smeared window at a rocky, gloomy, treeless glen. Its sparse grass and heather couldn't tempt so much as a black-faced sheep. Beside a nearby bog a rusty Scottish Tourist Board sign of crossed broadswords marked the Battle of Glen Whatever, way back in Seventeen Forget-It. Ahead, around a bend in the road, was a bridge. The burn was in spate but well below road level.

'What's the problem?' someone called.

'Water-horse,' said the driver.

'A kelpie?' cried an American passenger. 'Wow, can we get out? Like, to film it?'

'No,' said the driver.

There was a clunk as the door locked, followed by a mutter of disappointment and a surge to my side of the bus. Phones were pressed to all the windows, including one quite rudely over my shoulder. I shrugged the overbearing arm aside and wiped the inside of the window with my sleeve, tilting my face and phone to a view of where the burn gushed from a gully half-way up the hillside.

At first it seemed nothing but one of the many small waterfalls and rapids on that eroded slope. Suddenly the water rose, brown and white, shouldering above the cleft in which it ran. The long roan head formed first, a black-eyed gleam, the white spume of the mane, and then the forelegs trampled air as the kelpie reared. Everyone – all the visitors, anyway – gasped, to a staccato of shutter-sounds. The kelpie waited, gathering water and strength. Then down it plunged, its speed and balance impossible, its gait a perfect gallop, tail and mane flying out behind it, boulders and bushes flung from its path. It over-leapt and flooded across the bridge, dislodging one or two stones from the parapet.

The water drained from the road. After a minute the driver got out and heaved the stones to the side. Passengers edged back to their seats. The engine started up. As we crossed the bridge we gazed down the watercourse, but the kelpie was long out of sight and by now probably prancing in the sea.

The bus lurched over the lip of the glen and sped across a boggy moor. Civilisation hove into view as a huddle of houses, a clump of rowans and a distant shaggy cow – and with them, 4G coverage again at last. I took my phone from the bag on my knees and tapped Maps. Twenty miles to go. Like most of the other non-locals on the bus, I took the opportunity to share my (disappointingly blurry) kelpie pics. Likes pinged in.

The view opened out, to a two-lane highway along a grassy plain between two ranges of hills. Ahead, through the arcs of the wipers, I could see a brighter sky and a glimmer of sea. Beyond it rose the craggy skyline of the Isle of Skye, a fainter grey against the clouds. We passed small farms, broad meadows, houses and ruins, clumps of woodland. The hiss of the tyres on the wet road and the whump of the wiper blades were almost louder than the thrum of the engine.

A few minutes later the road took us along the coast. We passed the grim block of Dornie Castle – you'll have seen it in *Highlander* – then climbed over a rise and swung left around the head of the loch. The roadside filled up with hotels and houses and a petrol station. Dinghies and sailboats bobbed, moored to buoys. The traffic thickened. The bus turned off the main road just after the sign for Kyle of Lochalsh and slowed to a crawl. The blink of sun vanished as another heavy cloud dragged its train of rain in from the west.

Kyle is a little town with narrow streets piled higgledy-piggledy on slopes and a cliff. Its most prominent features are the slipway, the railway station, and two great grey naval fuel tanks. After ten minutes of manoeuvring to avoid streets choked by the ferry queue, the coach pulled up near the slipway at a car park open to the elements. I put away the compact with which I'd hastily checked my make-up, stood up, tugged my cagoule from the overhead rack, and joined the shuffle forward and then the huddle around the driver as he heaved luggage from the hold. Rain rattled on my hood. I grabbed my rolling case and the bulky, heavy sports bag containing my books and walking boots and trainers and fleece and jumpers and (a wry thought at this moment) swimming gear, slung the shoulder bag containing (among other things) my precious laptop over a forearm, and hurried to the pier.

This being summer, the wind wasn't exactly cold, but it was strong and rainy enough to go straight through the thin cheap trousers of the supermarket suit I'd bought at the last minute and which was already seeming less of a bargain. I tried to ignore the dribble from the hem of my cagoule onto the front of my legs. This wasn't so hard, because I felt quite exhilarated. Even with the rain spattering my face and rat-tailing the strands of hair that I couldn't stuff back into the hood, the air felt good: fresh in my nose and lungs, smelling of sea and seaweed and engines and carrying the cry of the gulls that hovered hopefully over the stern of the twenty-eight-car ferry approaching the quay. The boat swung around in a surge of foam as the screws went into reverse.

A few hundred metres away, across a choppy channel with

a strong tidal current, was my destination, Kyleakin. A scatter of houses around the slipway, and the ruin of a castle from which the remains of one tower poked like two upraised fingers from a clenched fist, were all I could see of it through the rain. The other ferry of the pair that plied this route was approaching the slipway at the far side – from where, as on the near, a line of cars and lorries wended out of sight. Likewise nearby were a few buses and coaches. In summer, the fare for coaches is prohibitive, so it's cheaper for the bus companies to run separate coaches on the island. By way of compensation, foot passengers travel free.

You'd think there'd be a bridge over the sea to Skye. There isn't. Whenever the project is mooted, some wise woman or aged seer or upstart wild-haired young prophet rouses themselves from crannog or bothan or sea-cave and hurries by bus and ferry and bus or train to the Scottish Parliament at Holyrood, and has a word. Shortly afterwards, the Skye Bridge proposal disintegrates in a flurry of withdrawn Green Papers and hasty disavowals of ever having been on the committee.

So there's still a car ferry across the narrow channel between Kyleakin and Kyle of Lochalsh. It's the rustic mystics who do the talking, but it's the selkies that everybody blames. Selkies are as set against sea-bridges as kelpies are against hydroelectric dams. There were grand schemes for Scottish hydroelectricity once. Back in the 1940s, the foundations for some dams were laid. You can see their ruins in the glens. In the Highlands and Islands, the electricity supply system is still called 'the Nuclear'.

The Kyleakin ferry's rusty, jointed steel ramp angled down, like finger-tips unfolding in a flourish from the wrist, and banged on the slipway. A crewman jumped from ferry to pier and made fast a rope at two bollards. The twenty-eight cars on board bumped off one by one. Twenty-eight cars were waved on board, one by one. Then the guy on deck beckoned the foot passengers. We crowded on either side into gangways that had a cover along the top, glass windows to the sea, and were open to the deck. Shelter depended on which way the wind was blowing.

I'd picked the unlucky side. I turned my back to the wind and gazed out at the sea. The ramp clanged up and curved over. The engine note shifted. The ferry backed away from the quay and swung around. Rain blurred the window. I turned around to the deck.

A tall young man in a blue jumper and jeans was going from car to car, taking fares. He had curly black hair that blew about in the wind. That was the first thing I noticed. The second was the way he moved. There was nothing flashy about it, no dancer's step, just a sure foot on the wet deck. And unlike everyone else on board, including the other crewman I'd seen, he didn't notice the rain. I don't mean he ignored it – that would have implied some effort. He just didn't notice it.

He noticed me. He straightened up from a rolled-down window where he'd just stooped to take a fare, and looked straight at me across the car roof, at a distance of a couple of metres. He had very blue eyes and a handsome, slightly brown face.

I felt something like an electric shock. I must have blinked.

He smiled, a flash of white teeth. He turned and moved to the next car, and didn't look back.

I stopped staring after him and moved further in, and found myself in front of a big laminated poster giving the company's conditions of passage. To distract myself from whatever was still making my knees shake, I read it. It listed all the misadventures for which the company took no responsibility in any circumstances. Among these were:

> *Delay. Loss of luggage. Theft of luggage by the company's servants. Arrival at a different destination to that advertised on the manifest. Injury or loss of life. Attack by Barbary pirates. Sale of cargo or luggage to Barbary pirates. Sale of passengers to Barbary pirates. War, conventional. War, nuclear. Travel through radioactive fallout. Diversion to avoid radioactive fallout. Terrorism. Counter-terrorism. Asteroid impact. Orders from established governments, or their civil and military servants. Actions or orders of strike committees. Actions or orders of committees of workers, farmers, soldiers, and intellectuals. Loss or damage caused by whales or monsters of the deep.*

That sample, by no means comprehensive, is not exaggerated. You can look at the list yourself, if ever you travel on a ferry in the Western Isles.

One thing is definitely not on it:

Complete, sudden, inexplicable loss of heart to complete stranger.

No, that's not on the list.

I checked.

I glanced over my shoulder as I paced down the ramp. I didn't see him. Rain still pelted. I hurried up the slipway, past the waiting queue of cars and the coaches. To my left was a small natural harbour, full of boats, with the ruined castle overlooking it. Hefting my shoulder bag, trundling my rolling case, and blinking the rain from my eyelashes, I headed into the village with as much dignity and poise as I could muster. I remembered where The Crossing Lodge was – third turning up from the pier on the left. I was still walking past cars full of restive children, and harried drivers standing in the rain for a quick smoke, when I turned off.

The Lodge was a solid two-storey stone-built detached villa with a small front garden, and two big bay windows. Projecting from the slope of the roof were three skylights under little roofs of their own. The sign outside said VACANCIES.

I put my bags down in the shelter of the porch and pressed the bell button beside the inner, half-glass door. After a few seconds I heard footsteps in the hall and the door opened. Standing there smiling out at me: a woman not much older than my mother. Her cheeks were ruddy and her eyes bright brown. Her hair, brown with a few white streaks, was piled on top of her head. She wore a floral-print apron over a white eyelet blouse and grey cardigan and black mid-calf skirt.

'Hello!' she said, stepping back. 'You must be Siobhan! Come right in, you look soaked.'

'Good afternoon, Mrs McIntyre,' I said. 'Thank you.'

I took off my cagoule and shook the water from it onto the path, away from the step. She gave me an approving look as I put down my bag and stood my case. She shook hands, and hung my cagoule from a stand by the door. The hallway smelled of furniture polish and wood varnish. Doors opened off to left and right, and the hall continued past a stairwell towards a kitchen at the back, glimpsed through a half-open door.

'Well now, Siobhan, I can see you need a nice hot *strupag*, but first you need to get out of those wet things before you catch your death.'

'Oh, I'll be fine,' I said, the cup of tea striking me as the much more urgent need, and pneumonia as no immediate danger.

Mrs McIntyre ignored me.

'Mairi!' she yelled down the hall. 'Get a wee pot of tea on!'

A faint sound came back.

'Now, let me show you to your room.' She gestured towards the stairs. 'It's right up in the attic, I'm afraid.'

'Oh, that's not a problem, Mrs McIntyre.'

'Now, now, Siobhan – call me Jeanie for goodness sake, everybody else does.'

She picked up my case. I took my shoulder bag and sports bag. Up we went, past a landing with ships in bottles on the windowsill, then along a carpeted corridor past fresh-painted doors to a steeper stairway at the back of the house. I climbed carefully, holding onto the handrail, and emerged into a bright and airy converted attic lit by skylights. Three doors opened from it.

'The one at the end,' Jeanie said, handing me a key.

The bedroom was small, but it had its own south-facing skylight window right ahead of me, and white-painted walls. The bed was a narrow double, with a dresser table and wooden chair across from it. A bowl of pot-pouri on the dresser filled the air with a magnolia scent. One door opened to a wardrobe, the other to the en suite. All the soft furnishings were of white eyelet cotton, some of it frilled.

'It's very nice!' I said, insincerely.

'I'm glad you like it,' said Jeanie, with a tight smile. 'You'll be keeping up to ten rooms as neat as this every day.'

'I'm sure I can manage,' I said.

'Och, I know you can,' said Jeanie. 'Make yourself at home.' She waved a hand around and backed out. 'No need to dress up again. Just pull on something casual, and for heaven's sake, dry! See you downstairs in the sitting-room.'

When I opened the wardrobe to put my suit jacket on a hanger I found half a dozen tabards and aprons, folded and stacked on box shelves labelled: 'chambers & laundry', 'kitchen', and 'tables'.

No chance of any workwear faux pas, then! I pulled on jeans and trainers, sent my mum a quick text and 'xxx', plugged my laptop in to recharge, gave my hair a shake in front of the wall mirror, and headed downstairs.

In the sitting-room sat Jeanie in an armchair, tea-tray on the coffee-table. In the bay of the window stood a guy about my own age in a chef's white coat, blue work trousers and thick-soled black boots. He had buzz-cut dark brown hair, slim features under a beginner's attempt at designer stubble. A girl who looked about sixteen perched on a low stool. She had a blond pony-tail, and wore jeans and a black and red death metal T-shirt. Her sulky look changed to a forced smile as she glanced towards me.

'Hello again, Siobhan,' said Jeanie. She waved towards the others. 'Gordon, Mairi.'

I shook hands with both. Over the pleased-to-meet-yous, Jeanie explained:

'Gordon's going to be cooking dinners from tomorrow, and Mairi's going to be serving at the dinner tables, she already comes in to serve breakfast. You'll be helping her with both if necessary. Now, sit yourself down and let Mairi practice pouring tea.'

Mairi shot her a dark look.

There were too many armchairs. The walls were hung with black-and-white or sepia photos of the Cuillins and black houses and toiling crofters and fishing-boats, and here and there with framed cross-stitches and tapestries. A grandfather clock in a walnut case ticked out the seconds, and showed the time as half past five, only a minute off. Tea-trolleys and corner tables and a bureau and a tapestry frame with half-finished project stood against the walls. The table had a scatter of newspapers – *The Press and Journal*, the *West Highland Free*

Press, the *Telegraph* – and women's and car and fishing magazines. Alcove shelves on either side of the fireplace held coffee-table books and thick battered paperbacks with pastel-coloured or foil-lettered spines, with a dozen Mills & Boons and two or three Penguins squeezed in among them.

'I see you're a reader,' said Jeanie, as Mairi finished pouring and settled down with her own cup.

'Well, yes,' I admitted. 'I'm a student.'

'So are we,' said Mairi, brightening. 'I'm still at school, but I want to get into nursing training, and Gordon's learning to be a chef.'

'And what are you studying yourself?' Gordon asked.

'I'm not sure yet,' I replied. 'I've just finished first year Arts at Glasgow Uni and I've done English, Moral Philosophy, and Biology. But I've been finding Biology so interesting – well, I've always been interested in marine biology anyway – that I'm thinking of switching to a science degree next academic year.'

'You've come a long way,' said Gordon. 'Are there no summer jobs in Glasgow?'

'Now, now,' said Jeanie, 'I'm sure Siobhan has more reasons than that to come here.'

'Well actually,' I said, 'that's part of it. I was so caught up in my exams that I forgot to get a job lined up before the end of the term. But yes, Jeanie, you're right, I wanted to come to somewhere nice and out of the city.'

Gordon laughed. 'And choked with traffic and crawling with tourists?'

The doorbell rang. Jeanie hustled us out and went to welcome a couple dripping on the doorstep. As I carried my cup and saucer and biscuit through to the kitchen, I reflected that I'd not told the whole truth.

I'd got out of Glasgow to avoid Kieran. He'd gazed moon-struck at me from a distance in Eng. Lang. and Lit. lectures for the first term, evidently made some New Year resolution and said hello in the spring term, and swept me entirely off my feet and into his bed. After two months of what for me was unalloyed happiness and walking on air, he'd delivered me a Very Serious Conversation in which he'd explained that he was dumping me because I was *too intense.* He'd then spent the next term with my former good friend Julia, among whose many retrospectively recognised faults even I couldn't include being too intense.

Kieran was one reason why I was thinking of switching to a science degree, because then I wouldn't meet him in second-year Eng. Lang. & Lit. The thought of Kieran was wiped from my mind by a sudden intense recollection of the ferry man's face.

I caught up with Mairi and Gordon, huddled from the continuing downpour under a little porch, smoking.

'Hi,' said Gordon. He held out a pack.

'No thanks,' I said. 'I need all my breath for swimming.'

'We take our chances when we can,' said Mairi, sucking hard. I considered pointing out that smoking was illegal at her age but guessed she might not be as young as she looked. Oh well – if she went on smoking, that problem would take care of itself.

'I'll have to be getting your dinner ready in a minute,' said Gordon.

'Oh, I didn't expect you to have to –'

'No problem at all,' he said. 'Practice run for tomorrow, anyway. Jeanie's overheard guests wishing they could have a bite here instead of eating out, so she decided to give it a go. Lamb chops, burgers, salmon or herring, black pudding, fresh peas and new potatoes, that sort of thing.'

'How about all of the above?' I said. 'Like, right now?'

Gordon laughed and tapped the side of his nose. 'I'll see what I can do.'

'And I'll do my waitress bit,' said Mairi. 'Try not to

laugh,okay?'

'Oh, I'll be a model customer,' I said.

'Aye, you'll be eating in the kitchen like us and Jeanie after tonight,' said Gordon. 'Making no promises there, mind.'

'Whatever's left over,' said Mairi. 'Scraps. Fishbone soup.'

I laughed. 'What do you do after work?'

'Sleep, I expect,' said Gordon.

'Is there any place you can go to have fun around here?'

'Depends what you mean by fun,' said Mairi, sounding bitter.

'Have a drink, relax, get some music…'

'Well,' said Mairi, 'there's two pubs. The Haakon's full of backpackers and the Old Castle's full of locals, or it used to be before –'

But at this point we heard a call from Jeanie. Gordon and Mairi flicked their cigarette-ends fizzing into puddles and hastened inside. I trailed after them. Jeanie didn't raise an eyebrow.

'Gordon,' she said, 'could you do me a favour? The new guests would be grateful if they could have dinner here tonight, and it's so wet out, I thought, for the goodwill… so would you mind?'

'Och, no problem,' said Gordon.

'Thanks!' said Jeanie. She glanced at me. 'Join me in the dining room in ten minutes?'

'Oh, yes please.'

She took off her apron and hung it up at the back of the kitchen door. Without it she looked like a businesswoman, her cardigan as shaped as a suit jacket.

'I'll just go and freshen up a wee bit,' she said. 'You're fine yourself. See you in a mo.'

Mairi, Gordon and I looked at each other after she'd left.

'Can I help here with anything?' I asked.

'Not tonight,' said Gordon, squatting in front of the

cooker. He opened the oven door and turned on the gas, peering inside until the flame flared up, then nudged the door shut with his toe. He picked up half a dozen A5 sheets and handed them to me.

'Well, you can help by putting these on the tables,' he said. 'Then sit down, look at the menu, and wait for Jeanie to join you and Mairi to come through and ask you if you'd like a drink while you're waiting.'

I refrained from pointing out that he seemed to be picking up Jeanie's micromanaging ways.

I sipped orange juice and chatted awkwardly with Jeanie until our dinners arrived. The guest couple were served first. I'd chosen what looked like the most challenging meal on the menu, Gordon's *piece de resistance*: herring, haggis and nettle fishcakes. It was a success. After dinner the guests and Jeanie went through to the living-room, where Jeanie answered questions about local attractions and I turned over pages of the local papers. At 7.25 everyone else, including Mairi and Gordon, agreed to watch EastEnders. I excused myself in the nick of time and went up to my room.

I unpacked and hung up in the wardrobe my clothes and drysuit. I piled my walking boots, face-mask, flippers and snorkel on the wardrobe floor, alongside four pairs of shoes.

That left my books: *Collins Pocket Guide to the Sea Shore*, Hume's *A Treatise of Human Nature*, and George Eliot's *The Mill on the Floss* – all advance reading for my second year. I set them in a neat row on the table, beside my phone and laptop and a hefty A4 spiral-bound notebook. More than enough reading for study, but… I had a dark suspicion I'd be hitting the chick-lit and thrillers and Penguins and at a pinch the Mills & Boons before the summer was over.

I took a picture out the window of the rain-lashed, darkening scene, uploaded it to Twitter and Instagram with a wry comment, and checked my messages. After answering these I caught up on Facebook. At nine-thirty I went back downstairs. Jeanie was in the living-room on her own, sitting at the bureau with a laptop and working through a stack of paper, while half-watching the telly.

'I think I'll have an early night,' I said.

She looked up, smiling. 'You have an early start. Six, I'm afraid.'

Shit, I thought.

'Oh, I'm fine with that,' I said.

'Sleep well.'

'You too.' I waved goodnight and hurried upstairs to shower and wash and dry my hair.

In the shower I felt something grainy under my feet, and looking down saw a scatter of sand on the bottom of the stall. I sluiced it away but as I was rinsing my hair I felt gritty grains on my scalp, and washed them vigorously out.

Must have been carried on the wind.

Two

I was swimming naked in water warmer and clearer than any I'd ever swum in, down to a rusty shipwreck. Someone was swimming just behind and above me. Our two shadows raced across the rippled sand of the seafloor below. Bright fish darted away from me and, beyond arm's length, hovered in the water, observing me with their cold round eyes.

Quite suddenly, I realised that I didn't have a face-mask, and that I had been holding my breath for some time. There was a persistent ringing in my ears. I needed to breathe. I was far, far below the surface. I twisted upward and started thrashing towards the distant shining wavy ceiling high above. My lungs ached to expel stale air, and to draw breath. Up and up I swam, and the surface seemed no nearer. Out of nowhere drifted a huge clump of brown bladder-wrack, entangling me in its slimy embrace. I struggled and struggled, becoming ever more desperate and confined. The ringing in my ears grew louder by the second. The pain in my chest became unbearable. Without any conscious decision I surrendered to the reflex, and breathed out. Bubbles wobbled upward in front of my face, great silvery squirming shapes, rising towards that surface now forever out of reach.

With an awful sense of finality and desolation I breathed in, and woke.

Sunlight beamed through thin curtains. The alarm on my phone blared from the bedside table. I freed my arm from a tangle of sheet and blanket and switched it off. The time was 5:32. The bedding had got wrapped around me. The nightmare had already begun to disintegrate like snowflakes on water.

I wriggled out of the entanglement and struggled out of bed. I felt sticky. I'd now have to take another shower, which hadn't been part of my plans. I rushed to the en suite, bundled my hair into a shower cap, and had a hasty sluice. I'd just finished towelling and was brushing my hair when I heard a knock on the door.

'Yes?' I called out.

'There's a mug of tea outside,' said Jeanie, through the door. 'A wee bit of breakfast in the kitchen in ten minutes!'

'Oh, thanks!' I called back. I half-dressed, ducked around the side of the door and picked up the mug. It had had time to cool a bit so I gulped it faster than usual, then scrambled into the sort of white and black combo I hadn't worn since school. I checked the Post-It labels for 'chambers & laundry' and snapped on a blue nylon tabard, paused to not admire the resulting look in the mirror, and hurried downstairs.

The kitchen smelled of tea, toast, coffee (ah!) and frying bacon, despite the half-open back door and the extractor fan roaring above the cooker. Jeanie and Mairi were sitting at the big table, scoffing fried eggs, toast, black pudding, and bacon rashers.

'Good morning,' I said. 'Thanks again for the tea.'

Jeanie waved towards the cooker. 'Help yourself,' she said. 'There's buttered toast in the oven.'

I helped myself to a couple of bacon rashers and slices of toast, poured a coffee and sat down. Jeanie gave my plate an anxious look.

'Are you sure that's all you'll be having?'

'Mmm, yes, it's fine,' I said. 'I usually just have some fruit and cereal.'

'Oh, that's okay, you can have that afterwards,' Jeanie said. 'But you really should have some more, an egg or something at least.'

'I'll be fine, really.'

Guests were already on the move, some checking out, and the guests' breakfast time started at 6:30.

'Now,' Jeanie said, glancing unnecessarily at her watch, under a wall clock ten past six, 'if you take the orders from the early risers, Mairi, I'll show Siobhan the ropes and then I'll be down to get cooking.'

I finished my coffee and followed Jeanie upstairs.

'Now the best place to start,' she said, 'is your own room.'

'What?' I said, as she flung its door open. 'But it's in a terrible mess, and –'

'Och, this is nothing,' Jeanie said, giving it a critical sweeping glance. 'You'll have it fresh as new in no time.'

I hauled off the tangle of bedding and piled it on the chair, added the pillows to the heap, and smoothed out the bottom sheet.

'Not the way at all,' said Jeanie, and proceeded to set me right.

'Okay,' Jeanie said at last, after a very long ten minutes. She handed me a bunch of keys. 'Room three have checked out. It's just off the next landing. Strip and replace – I'll show you the cupboard.'

There I was introduced to an arsenal of cleaning liquids and a vacuum-cleaner with cheery eye decals, which I mentally dubbed Mr Sucky.

For the next two hours I dealt with the bedrooms, followed by laundry and more cleaning in the other rooms and passageways. I acquired a deep loathing for the smell of Pledge. Finally it was two o'clock. Jeanie made me a sandwich and a mug of soup, and told me I had the rest of the afternoon off.

'But I'll need you back for 5.30,' she said. 'We have five tables at dinner tonight.'

My upper arms were aching. I ran up the stairs to my room, washed, changed into T-shirt and jeans, dropped my phone in my shoulder-bag, and headed out.

The day was warm and sunny, with a cool breeze smelling of sea and heather. Just my luck – if I'd travelled one day later I'd have had a much more pleasant and interesting journey up from Glasgow, with blue skies and spectacular views instead of rain.

But then I might not have seen the kelpie, or have met the ferry man's glance.

I strolled down to the main road and turned right, towards the ferry. I found the queue about a hundred yards on, and walked past the vehicles to the harbour. The ferry boats were passing each other halfway across the narrow channel. Near the foot of the slipway were half a dozen backpackers, a man with a muddy mountain bike, and a couple of local ladies with shopping bags, waiting for their free ride across to Kyle.

I hadn't made any decision about where I was going. I hadn't had to. There never was any question in my mind that I'd go to the ferry, and that I'd look for the guy I'd seen the day before. If I didn't see him on the way over, I'd see him on the way back. And if I didn't see him today, I'd see him tomorrow. Or the day after.

I didn't look at the ferry as it came in. I gazed down into the water. Small fish darted amid clumps of kelp, and jellyfish pulsed helplessly close to the shingle and their doom.

The ramp clanged down. Engines coughed up. I followed the other foot passengers on board, and made my way towards the far end. The ramp there was up and the walkway ended in a white-painted, bolted gate. After a couple of minutes a hooter sounded, and the other ramp cranked up and clanked into place. The ferry pulled away from the quay. The landscape swung around us like a camera pan. The ferry was butting into the waves with blunt force that sent spray onto my face and splashes far too close. I moved a little farther back down the walkway, looking at the stubby castle and the craggy shore.

Then I turned around and started scanning for the guy. I could see two of the crew. One was in the wheelhouse, the other collecting fares. Neither was the guy I'd shared that glance with yesterday. Maybe I'd taken the wrong boat. I took a few steps farther down the walkway, looked around again, and paused to gaze out at the sea.

'Excuse me,' someone said, from behind my shoulder.

I turned, and there he was. He was more than a head taller than me so I found myself first looking at his chest and inhaling the smell of fresh sea air and hot engine oil off his jumper, then looking up, straight into his bright blue eyes. Again I felt a jolt, and actually recoiled back against the railing. In each hand he held a grubby, steaming mug of strong-smelling black tea.

'Sorry,' he said, with a smile, as he edged sideways past me. His trainers were scuffed to bits. He began to turn away. This didn't strike me as something I could let happen.

'Your turn for the galley?' I asked, saying the first thing that had popped into my head.

He glanced over his shoulder.

'The kettle cupboard, more like,' he said.

This banal exchange felt exciting because it didn't seem like the first time we'd spoken. It was as if we'd known each other for years. Even the casual way he looked back at me and the half-smile he flickered before turning away again thrilled me with its familiarity. Then he was off across the deck, handing one mug to the guy who'd just finished collecting fares, then bounding up the steps to the wheelhouse, all without splashing a drop.

I didn't see him the rest of the crossing. The ferry hove to at the Kyle slipway. I made my way off, letting the backpackers and shopping ladies go first, and walked past the long queue of cars. The air was heavy with vanilla from all the ice-creams being dripped by waiting children – a van parked a bit up the road had a long queue of its own. I stopped at the top of the slipway and glanced back. I saw the guy strolling up it, about twenty metres behind me. He smiled and nodded. I waited. He stopped a few metres away.

'Hello,' he said.

'Hello again,' I said.

'Are you going for a walk?'

'Yes,' I said.

He looked away, then back. 'Would you like to walk with me around the shore a wee bit? I'm on my way to the fishing-boat pier, to pick up some fish.'

'Oh yes!' I said. 'Please!'

He gave such a relieved smile that I felt a lurch inside. *He* was shy about *me?*

'Okay,' he said. He stuck his hands in his jeans pockets and stepped towards me, looking down. 'Well.' He glanced up, jerking his head at a junction across the road. 'It's over that way.'

We threaded our way through the cars, and onto a street down towards another stony beach. He walked alongside me rather than with me, half a metre or so out of my space, not looking at me.

Tongue-tied too? Hah!

'So what's your name?' I asked, brightly.

'I'm Cal,' he said. 'Cal Mac.' That's what it sounded like.

I laughed. 'Like the ferry?'

'Short for Calvin Mack,' he said.

'MacWhat?' I asked.

'M-A-C-K,' he spelled out.

'Oh!' I said, remembering the only place I'd come across that surname. 'Like in *The Testament of Gideon Mack*.'

'What's that?'

'It's a novel I read last winter. It's kind of dark, about a minister who's an atheist and who meets the Devil, Old Nick himself.'

'Who's it by?'

'James Robertson, he's –'

'Aye,' he said. 'I've heard of him.' He laughed. 'It's a funny thing, you know, why the British called the Devil "Old Nick".'

'I've never thought of that,' I said, feeling that the conversation was very much going my way, if at a tangent. 'So why did they?'

'After Niccolo Machiavelli,' he said. 'You know? Author of *The Prince*.'

'Oh, right,' I said.

'Have you read it?' he asked.

'Yes. It was in English.'

'No, it was in Italian.'

'I mean I read it in English Literature. Or maybe in Moral Philosophy. This year, anyway.'

'Ah!' he said, looking pleased. 'You're a student!'

'Yes,' I said, feeling defensive. 'I'm here on a summer job.'

'Nothing wrong with being a student.'

'I didn't think there was,' I said. 'What about you?'

'What about me?'

'Are you a student?'

I'd walked a few steps before I realised he wasn't still in the corner of my eye. I turned. He was standing still, frowning into the distance. After a moment he shook his head.

'No,' he said. 'I'm not a student. I work on the boats. But I read a lot.'

'That's good,' I said, then felt it might have sounded patronising.

'Oh, it's good,' he said. 'It's good all right.'

He caught up with me in a couple of brisk strides. 'But yon Machiavelli wasn't as much of a devil as they make out,' he said, seriously. 'He used to dress up in his court clothes. In front of a mirror, would you believe? Mirrors were rubbish in those days.' He sounded as if he was thinking of complaining to the management. 'Anyway, old Nick used to pose and talk to himself as if he still had an audience with the Pope or the Duce or whoever. Giving them advice, you know? And then he'd scribble it all down. That's what it all came from – *The Prince*. Huh!'

'You seem to take it very personally,' I said.

He shot me a worried look. 'Oh, it's not that,' he said. He seemed to hunch over a bit more. I got the impression he wanted to kick pebbles. 'I'm not educated,' he said, with an odd intensity, still mooching along. 'It's all reading Penguin Classics and that. They sort of smear out into one time.'

'Uh huh,' I said, not quite with him.

He straightened, suddenly, and took his hands from his pockets and let his arms swing. He looked tall and confident, like when I'd first seen him.

'I've told you my name,' he said, and smiled. 'And I haven't asked you yours.'

'Siobhan Ross,' I said.

'Good to meet you.'

He crossed his arms in front of him and pulled off his jumper, slinging it around his shoulders as he walked. A blue singlet revealed his muscular arms and chest. His tan didn't go below his neck or above his elbows: he must have got it working, not sunbathing. This thrilled me.

We walked on in silence to the wooden pier that jutted from where the road ran parallel to the shore. A fishmonger's van was parked beside the near end, and a couple of open boats were tied up at the other. Three men lugged ice-filled crates of fish and lobsters from the boats to the van. The van's generator thumped steadily, presumably to power its refrigeration.

Cal gave me a nod and a glance, and ambled onto the long rickety pier to the boats. He exchanged words and coins, and returned with a plastic shopping bag weighted with half a dozen mackerel, still just about alive. Here and there their spiny fins had pricked the plastic.

Cal hoisted the bag, grinning.

'Tonight's tea for the crews,' he said.

'Where do you cook them?' I asked, as we set off back up the road.

'A wee camping gas ring.'

'Sounds good,' I said. 'I had herring fish-cakes last night.'

He chuckled. 'Working in a B&B?'

'That's right,' I said. 'Making beds, cleaning rooms and waiting tables at The Crossing Lodge.'

'I know the one,' he said.

'I've got to be back at work at 5:30,' I said.

'I've got to be back in five minutes!'

'When do you finish work?' I asked, feeling rather blatant.

'Ten tonight,' he said.

'Good grief!' I said.

'It's the summer.'

We'd reached the top of the road and were now going back down towards the ferry pier, and the end of the queue was already behind us.

'I can see that,' I said.

'I work twelve-hour shifts sometimes,' he went on. 'I could

work longer, but it's not allowed.'

'EU regulations? Union rules?'

'Factories Act,' said Cal.

'Like, the nineteenth-century one?'

'Aye, as amended. But I've got early starts and early finish tomorrow and Friday.'

I instantly wondered if this was a hint that we could meet after he finished work. But instead of asking outright, I just said: 'I expect I'll finish about nine, most evenings.'

'Yes,' he said, nodding. 'Hard work and long days, that's what you'll have this summer.'

I didn't know what to say to this sympathetic-sounding but unhelpful and unhopeful response, so I said nothing. As we neared the slipway, Call pulled his jumper back on, deftly passing the bag from hand to hand as he did so. The ferry was a hundred metres out, having been across and back while we'd been to the fishing pier. We walked down to the top of the slipway and waited for it to come in. I looked down, into the water and at the sea-anemones opening and closing below the tide-line. Cal looked out across the narrow channel, shading his eyes.

'I'm seeing a sail out there,' he said.

I peered into the glare and didn't see any sail. What I saw looked more like a fin: a huge black tilted rectangle sticking out of the water above the long curved back of a sea-monster.

'A submarine!' I cried.

'Yes,' said Cal. 'A Royal Navy nuclear submarine, Astute class.'

'So why did you say "a sail"?'

He gave me a puzzled frown. 'That's what it's called. The, uh…' He snapped his fingers. 'The conning tower! But submariners and sailors call it the sail.'

'And which are you?' I asked, feeling bold again. 'A sailor, or a submariner?'

'Och, I'm just a ferry man,' he said. 'You wouldn't catch me going in one of those things, oh no.' He was still gazing at it, as it slid on up the channel between the mainland and the island, doing quite a rate of knots. 'As for being a sailor, well, I've sometimes given it thought, but I doubt they'd have me.'

'Why not?' I asked.

He looked at me sidelong, smiling. 'You could say I don't have the qualifications.'

I was about to ask him why he couldn't study for the qualifications when the ramp rang down on the slipway and he was gone, leaping onto the deck without ado or goodbye. He launched himself off the slipway from a standing start, soared across a four-metre gap like Nijinsky, and landed on the ball of one foot straight in a puddle and in the half-metre gap between a car and the bulkhead at the side of the deck. He didn't slip, although – as I could see as he jumped – the soles of his trainers were worn smooth. It was an extraordinary leap, hair-raisingly dangerous, probably forbidden by the Factories Act let alone the Health and Safety at Work Act. Then he danced off up that narrow gangway, swinging the plastic bag above his head like a trophy. He disappeared through a hatch in the superstructure in the middle of the ferry.

I stared after him, as a score of cars and a lorry banged and rumbled off the boat. I didn't know what to think. I wasn't sure whether or not to just turn around. I glanced at my watch. The time was half past three. Not too late to take a proper walk along the shore, or to have a wander around Kyle's narrow streets.

After a minute's swithering, I joined the stream of foot passengers boarding the ferry. I made my way to the same spot as I'd been in before. The submarine had crossed the ferry's route to head up the channel. Its size was evident as its sail passed the stubby ruined castle.

The ramp clanged up and the ferry pulled away, wake

churning. The sea breeze cooled my face. Someone jostled past me – a back-packer with binoculars. I heard cameras giving the click sound-effect. The submarine and the coast could be a dramatic picture.

I pulled out my phone and thumbed to the camera.

'That's funny,' I heard someone say. 'It's stopped moving.'

'It's just the perspective,' said an American voice.

'Perspective my ass,' said another. 'It's run aground.'

I peered across dazzling reflections, wishing I had my sunglasses. The black silhouette of the sub's fin wavered in heat-haze. I zoomed in. This magnified the wavering, but made clear that the boat had indeed stopped. Tiny figures emerged on deck, and on the top of the conning tower. A signal flag was run up. I clicked away, and zoomed back to get some shots framed as I'd originally intended.

The ferry swung around, fighting the current, and the submarine passed out of sight behind the headland. I put the phone back in the bag.

Just as I was leaving the ferry, deflated and wondering what there was to do for an hour or so in Kyleakin, Cal stepped out on the ramp in front of me.

'I was wondering if you might maybe like to meet for a drink tomorrow evening,' he said.

'Oh!' I said. 'Um, yes. Where?'

He glanced up toward the top of the slipway. 'There?' he said.

'Yes!' I said. 'I'll meet you right there just after nine tomorrow, then.'

He smiled, again in such a relieved and grateful way that it gave me butterflies. I felt like flinging my arms around him right then and there, but didn't.

'See you, then,' he said.

'Count on it,' I said.

He waved, and sprang to the slipway to deal with the rope,

and didn't look back. I marched up the slipway grinning all over my face.

By now it was quarter to four, and I had an hour or so to kill. I turned left and headed along the little street parallel to the shore. This street had a few small shops, some for tourists and some for locals. I looked into the first, a newsagent's that doubled as a general store, stocked with emergency groceries and small jars of instant coffee. I bought the day's *Guardian* and wandered on.

A couple of doors along was a Broadford Hospital Trust charity shop. I nodded to the spry old lady behind the counter, and browsed bookshelves. Romances, chick-lit, cookery books, war novels, and Christian and pagan spirituality. I found an old *Observer's Book of Sea and Seashore* for a pound, and pounced on it like a gull on a chip wrapper. The clothes racks offered extensive ranges of dowdy, wintry, or children's, but again I made a good discovery: a flared floral tiered skirt in my size and last summer's style. At three pounds it was a bargain, and it seemed to be a good omen, so I bought it. I glanced at my watch as I awaited change of a fiver, and saw that forty minutes had gone by. (These 'missing time' episodes in charity shops and bookshops are a paranormal phenomenon. Someone should investigate.)

'Oh,' said the old lady, handing over a pound and sticking my purchases in a much-reused M&S carrier bag. 'You must be that Siobhan who's working up at Jeanie's place.'

I stared at her. 'How do you know that?'

'Och, they say you're a marine biologist, and that wee book…'

'Excuse me, but who's "they"?'

'People who come in,' she said, waving vaguely.

'Oh, fine,' I said. 'See you again soon.'

She smiled. I smiled and went out. As I closed the door behind me I noticed she had an open laptop beside the till and was already tapping at it. I'd expected village life to be more gossipy and less anonymous than Glasgow, but not wired Miss Marples.

I walked on, checking the windows of a couple of tourist shops – one tartan tat, the other local crafts – and the pub at the far end, the Haakon's Arms. I glanced at the ruined castle, decided it could wait for another day, and turned around to head back to the Crossing Lodge. As I walked past the harbour I heard the heavy throb of helicopters, and looked up to see a big yellow Sea King arrive and hover just beyond the castle. Moments later a smaller, darker chopper came in from the east to begin a wide and wary circling. Rescuers in the first and reporters in the second, I guessed.

'Had a nice wee walk?' Jeanie asked, as she let me in.

'Oh yes!' I said. 'I took the ferry over to Kyle for a bit, and then had a wander along the street down at the harbour.' I flourished my shopping bag. 'Bought a skirt and a book in the charity shop.'

'Oh, very nice! Maggie's a dear, isn't she? I must make sure you get a front door key of your own, Siobhan, there's one or two spare. Wait a minute.'

She took a bunch of keys from her apron pocket, opened a cupboard door beside the stairs and came out with a key attached by hairy sisal to a fuzzy card. 'There you are now.'

'Thanks,' I said. 'Well, I'll just get ready.'

'You do that. See you in half an hour.'

'What's going on out there, by the way?' Jeanie asked as I had my foot on the second step. 'Was it helicopters I just heard?'

I looked back. 'It seems a sub's run aground behind the castle,' I said. 'It's the Coast Guard and STV or BBC overhead, I think.'

'Och my,' said Jeanie. 'Well, if they will keep doing that, no wonder…' She shook her head, and smiled up at me. 'Now that's just me being silly. Off you go.'

Off I went, up the stairs, wondering what she'd meant. She hadn't *said* anything silly. In my room I freshened up and changed into my work clothes, giving the new skirt a twirl along the way. I used my remaining fifteen minutes to text my mum and to send out a few Tweets. Then I put the phone in a drawer, hung up the charity-shop skirt in the wardrobe and took out one of the white square aprons and tied it on and slipped a notebook and pencil in the pocket. When I went downstairs and joined Mairi in taking orders and serving at tables. There were three groups for dinner at first, and another four arrived later. I managed to take down every order correctly and not to spill anything.

So when I sat down with Jeanie, Gordon and Mairi at 8:45 with the dishwasher humming and Gordon's quick dishes of salad and Stornoway black pudding in front of us I was feeling pretty good about everything.

'You did well,' Jeanie said. 'Seeing it was your first time.'

'Oh, thanks,' I said. 'Mairi kept me right.'

'And they really liked Gordon's dinners,' Mairi said.

'Mm-hmm,' I commented, mouth full.

Gordon grinned at us all. 'Working here is easy after the college kitchen. Talk about competitive. All these guys.'

'I thought you'd like that,' said Mairi, mischievously. Jeanie rolled her eyes.

'Any news on the submarine?' I asked, breaking the sudden

silence.

'Oh, yes,' said Jeanie. 'It was on the news. They waited for the high tide to float it off, but it's still stuck on a shoal.'

'Surely the shoal's marked on their charts?' I said.

'It should be,' said Jeanie. 'There'll be an inquiry, and a lot of red faces, just you wait.'

'No hurry getting it off,' said Gordon. 'It's becoming a tourist attraction in its own right. The shore was hoaching with people when I came in.'

'I might take a wander down myself,' I said, glancing out of the window. 'It's still light.'

'I'll come with you,' said Mairi.

'Sure,' I said.

'Don't let her drag you into the pub,' said Jeanie, smiling to show she didn't mean it as sternly as she sounded. She got up and hung her apron on a peg.

'Thanks again, all of you. Now I've got to update the accounts, while you lot go gallivanting.'

When she'd gone we all felt a bit more relaxed.

'What did you mean about the college kitchen?' I asked Gordon.

He snorted. 'It's a bear-pit. I blame celebrity chefs. All the other students are straight guys acting macho and shouting and swearing like troopers.'

'Aren't there any women on the course?'

'Yes, but not cooking. They go for sensible things like hotel management.'

'So,' I said, taking what Gordon had just said as a coming out to me, 'you're the only gay in the college, is that it?'

'Too bloody true,' he said. 'And on the island, it sometimes feels.'

He jumped up. 'Well, I have an experiment with very slow cooking to do, and it has to start now.'

He went over to the fridge and took out a massive leg of

mutton on a platter and began pouring olive oil and rubbing seasoning. Mairi and I finished up our dinners.

'Are you sure it's okay if I join you?' Mairi asked, looking worried.

'Of course, gosh, yes.'

'You didn't sound very enthusiastic when I –'

'Sorry,' I said. 'Bit preoccupied. I'd love to walk down to the shore with you, and maybe nip into a pub so long as we're not too late.'

'Oh, good!' She smiled, her face clearing.

'By the way,' I said, 'you were saying last night, about the pubs…?'

'Oh, yes,' said Mairi. 'Well, the Old Castle's the kind of local that's been nearly empty since the smoking ban, it's a sad place now, just limping along, with any evening just two or three old *bodaich* reminiscing about their glory days working for the Nuclear and wishing they could still have a pipe with their pints. And the Haakon, it's more touristy -- lots of woolly jumpers demanding brands of real ale that aren't on tap and giving their opinions on the ones that are. The music, well you might like it, it's all Gaelic and folky but a bit M-O-R for me.' She gazed moodily out the window for a moment, then brightened. 'Still, it's the only place here you're likely to meet a good-looking boy.'

'Aw, come on,' I said. 'Surely there's some local lads who're all right.'

'Aye, and they've all left!' said Mairi.

'To the bright lights,' said Gordon, 'and the jumping night life of Fort William.'

He gazed down at the mutton joint and reached for a jar. 'Come to think of it,' he added, 'any good-looking guys from Kyleakin, you've probably met them in Glasgow.'

'Oh, I don't know about that,' I said, sounding smug even to myself. 'I've already seen at least one local boy who's a knock-out. He works on the ferry. And – he asked me out for a drink tomorrow night!'

Mairi drew in a sharp breath. Gordon looked up from crumbling a pinch of herbs.

'Cal?' he said, with a laugh. 'You don't need to bother about him.'

'Why not?' I asked, trying to keep the dismay out of my voice. Was Cal taken, or married, or gay, or…?

'He's a selkie,' Gordon explained.

The bottom dropped out of my world.

Three

I saw a selkie once.

One hot summer holiday when I was about eight, I was swimming off Millport on the Isle of Cumbrae, with my first facemask and snorkel. Toys really, bought by my dad on the way to the sandy beach at the back of the harbour. They wouldn't last, but for now they worked. The water was cold, so I couldn't have stayed in for long, and the sun burned on my back. My father was in up to his chest, wading within reach of me. I splashed and gasped along at the surface, thrilled that I could see clearly and breathe with my face in the water. The sunlight converged wherever I looked, like spotlights directed just for me. I saw small fish amid swaying seaweed, and shrimps scuttling along the floor of the silent sea. Their legs sent up little puffs of shell-sand mud, and left dotted lines behind.

I wanted to look closer. I surfaced, waved to my father and took a deep breath. I closed my lips again around the snorkel's mouthpiece, and ducked under, swimming down about a metre or so. I could feel pressure on my ears, and swallowed hard. I turned my head up and looked ahead. Something about six metres away caught my eye.

What at first seemed like a long frond of loose seaweed

rippled through the water, just visible. At its leading end was an almost semicircular curve, which snaked into several longer, shallower curves. The shape it made was like an outline of the upper surface of someone swimming, and so was its movement. I stared, amazed, until I needed to breathe. I thrust upward and took a wave in my face. I trod water, spluttering, and cleared the snorkel and my nostrils. A quick glance over my shoulder at my father, then down I went again.

The long strap of seaweed now had at its front end a clump of green weed, drifting along like hair on the sketched swimmer's head – and, darting in the cup of the curve, a pair of small fish whose silver skin gleamed like eyes. Moments later, some tiny, flickering fish lined up like teeth in a smile. Two wriggling elvers arced to shape open lips around them.

And then, as if that outline had been suddenly filled in, the sea-life sketch was all replaced by a long-haired, naked, swimming man, looking straight at me and smiling. Attracted and alarmed, I swam upward to burst out of the water and turn toward my father. I took the snorkel from my mouth and clutched it in one hand as I swam as fast as I could towards him, then reached out my free hand and grabbed his. I blinked up at him through a facemask that had leaked a little around the edges.

'What's the matter, Siobhan?'

'There's a man swimming under the sea,' I said, taking the mask off and shaking drops out. 'He wasn't there before, there was just seaweed and fish.'

My father looked scared, which scared me.

'Perhaps we'd better go in,' he said.

'Y-yes,' I said, teeth chattering.

He waded towards the beach and I swam alongside him, feeling happier. Once or twice I saw him glance over his shoulder. My toes touched the bottom, then my knees. I stood up.

'Was the man you saw wearing scuba gear or anything like that?' my dad asked, as we waded ashore.

'No,' I said. I giggled as he wrapped me in a towel. 'He had no clothes on at all.'

'Ah,' said my father. 'Would you like an ice-cream cone?'

Years later I learned that I'd seen a selkie. Not until last year, in first-year biology, did I read anything scientific about selkies.

Taxonomically, the Metamorpha are a dustbin category, like a file labelled 'Other'. It includes other shape-shifting entities such as the Saharan dust-devil, the Transylvanian vampire, the Indonesian green-man, the Caledonian water-horse, and the Palaearctic forest wraith. Some have argued that it should include the cherubim, but all we know of the shape of cherubim is the three-metre-wide feathery imprints they leave when they collide with patio doors, and which (I speak from bitter teenage suburban experience) are an absolute pain to clean off. No evolutionary connection between Metamorpha, or between them and other clades, has ever been confirmed. No evolutionary precursors have been identified (though there are some troubling trace fossils in the Burgess Shale, a disputed mummified seal-form from the Rancho La Brea tar pits, and some humaniforms from the Siberian permafrost).

No experimental studies have been done since late Victorian and early Edwardian times, in that brief historical window after long-range harpoons had been invented and before people realised that there might be an ethical issue with using them on selkies. There are steel engravings of fishermen in Guernseys and bowlers, scientific gentlemen in frock-coats and top hats, and now and again ladies in bustles and bonnets, standing perilously in small open boats with bow-mounted harpoon guns, and gazing curiously at some poor specimen thrashing in a net. There are photographic plates of scientists in laboratories, delivering electric shocks to similar unfortunates strapped in rubberized canvas troughs and recording their shape-changes: seal, human, shoal of fish, stinking mess of algae – which last was burned to ash, the flame to the spectroscope, the ash to the balance.

This kind of study was increasingly pilloried by anti-vivisection agitators, and ended by the Cruelty to Animals Act of 1908. In the nick of time the Admiralty delivered an apology and an appeal to the selkies, at some secret conclave in 1910 off the coast of St Kilda (some of whose dwindling people knew how to summon them with songs, the story goes). The selkies turned out to be very helpful to the Royal Navy in the Battle of Jutland. In the Second World War unknown numbers saw action at Dieppe, mined the harbours at Caen and Cherbourg, and went ashore with the Royal Marines at Juno Beach. Since 1910, and even more since 1945, any scientific work with or on selkies has been military, and secret.

As far as open science goes, it's back to natural history: there's been the occasional population estimate, a few underwater camera observations – from Cousteau's pioneering work to Attenborough's characteristic tour de force of a close-up, his breathy voice even breathier in the scuba mouthpiece – and great deal of perplexed speculation. The usual explanation, or brush-off, is the extra-terrestrial (indeed, extra-solar) hypothesis, but there are still some scientists who seriously suggest that the Metamorpha come from (not a supernatural realm, of course, but) a *discontiguous spatial domain*, which sounds very much like a supernatural realm to me.

Anyway…

I gave Gordon a dismayed look and cried: 'How could you possibly know that?'

Gordon nudged a tap open with the heel of his hand and washed his greasy and bloody fingers, then turned to dry his hands on a clump of kitchen-roll.

'Well, I can't say for sure, obviously,' he said, tossing the paper towels in the bin. 'But it's the word in the village.'

'Gossip, you mean?' I said, snatching at a straw of hope.

Gordon looked away. 'That's all it ever can be,' he said. 'But…' He shrugged. 'It's what people *don't* say that matters. If you ask the ferry crew or the office, they'll tell you they can't tell you. That's as good as an admission.'

'Maybe to you!' I said. 'Have you asked them yourself?'

'No,' Gordon admitted. 'But I heard it from someone who did.'

'So that's just hearsay too –'

Mairi laid a hand on my arm.

'Siobhan, don't get so worked up about this. We should go out, come on, get some fresh air and we'll talk about it on the way down to the shore.'

'Okay,' I said. 'Okay. Sorry, Gordon.'

'No problem,' Gordon said, putting the joint in the fridge. He took off his white coat and headed for the back door. 'See you in the morning, ladies.'

I ran up to my room, scrambled out of the black skirt and into the new flowery one, threw on a jacket, grabbed my bag, and whirled downstairs. Mairi was waiting in the hall, having in the meantime somehow managed to change into skinny blue jeans and strappy gold flats, and freshen up her lips and eyelashes with new and more vivid colour, so that she looked not just older than she was but older than *me*.

She clocked me reading this and gave me cheeky grin.

'You're the one who'll get carded,' she explained as we went out the front door.

I had to laugh, despite my mind's still being in turmoil. At the gate, Mairi stopped to light a cigarette. We walked on. The sky was shading to green in the west, the sun still well above the horizon. The breeze off the sea was cool enough to make me glad of my jacket. The Sea King had flown off, but two small helicopters buzzed in the middle distance.

'Well,' said Mairi, 'isn't this grand!'

'Yes,' I said. 'Now, you were saying…'

'Oh yes!' She took a deep draw of her cigarette. 'About Cal, well, the thing is he turned up about, oh, two years ago, and started work on the ferry. He never said where he came from. He has a local accent, everyone here can tell he's from this part of the island, but nobody knows him. Not from school or anything. And nobody knows where he lives.'

She glanced sideways at me, and spoke almost out of the side of her mouth. 'One of my friends really fancied him, and being a wee daft lassie at the time she followed him after work, and she said he went around a corner up in the village and just disappeared. There's a dog just round that corner that barks when anyone goes by, and it didn't, until she turned the corner herself just seconds after Cal, and then the dog went mental. Cal was nowhere to be seen.'

'Well, that's me convinced,' I said. 'And has he lured any local lassies away to his kingdom under the sea?'

'No,' he hasn't,' Mairi admitted. 'He doesn't even have a girlfriend, though there's plenty have tried.'

'Maybe he's just waiting for the right one to come along,' I said, more cheerily than I felt.

'Oh, don't say that!' said Mairi.

'Why not?'

'It's sort of… tempting fate.'

I just laughed. Mairi tossed her cigarette-butt, stepped on it, and walked on in silence.

We turned right onto the street I'd explored that afternoon. Mairi led the way to the turn-off to the ruined castle, via a bridge over a shallow tidal creek. A dozen or so people were ahead of us, almost in single file. Along that path we traipsed, then over the shoulder of the mound, to come upon a view of the channel. The tussocky slope down to the rocky shore below us was crowded with fifty or so people, most with binoculars, some with tripod-mounted cameras or telescopes. All eyes and lenses were on the smooth black sinister shape of the submarine, less than a hundred metres away and mostly underwater apart from the fin and part of the deck, over which waves were breaking. A tugboat, and a bigger, industrial-looking vessel bristling with cranes, stood by. The racket of the helicopters overhead made it difficult to speak, or even to think.

Mairi took out her phone and started poking about on it. She laughed abruptly.

'What's funny?' I asked.

'State of this,' said Mairi. She showed me her phone. On the screen was an app with a map zoomed to where we stood. The tugboat and the larger vessel were clearly identified, as were passing craft, and the ferries. Of the submarine there was no trace.

'That's how secret subs are,' she said. 'They don't show up on Vessel Finder even when they're in plain sight.'

But, having seen the sub, there wasn't much else to see. After five minutes we looked at each other, shrugged, nodded, and headed back to the street.

'Well,' said Mairi, after we'd gone far enough away for the helicopter noise to retreat to an annoying background buzz, 'that was interesting – not! Now, do you fancy a wee drink before we go home?'

I glanced at my watch. Quarter to ten. The sky to the west

was reddening. The Haakon's Arms stood just across the road.

'Oh, yes, let's,' I said.

The pub's sign was a big picture of a grinning red-bearded Viking with a steel tiara riveted around the rim of his helmet, a chain-mailed barrel chest, and a beer-foaming horn clutched in his mighty fist. I suspected that the reference material for this representation had been a biker at a real ale festival.

We pushed through the swing door and found ourselves in a bar that looked Scandinavian, all strip-lighting and stripped pine. The sound-system played Karen Matheson singing in Gaelic, at a tolerable volume. A dozen or so people sat at tables and a few others leaned elbows on the bar. About half the people in here were indeed what Mairi had called 'woolly jumpers' (even if they weren't actually wearing woolly jumpers) and the others looked local.

'What would you like?' I asked Mairi.

'No, no, it's me,' she said. 'What are you having?'

'Oh, a dry white wine, please.'

She got a Chardonnay for me and a pint of lager for herself, and we sat down on the inbuilt benches behind a table in the corner. We clinked glasses, and sipped.

'So,' Mairi said, picking up where we'd left off, 'you don't believe Cal is a selkie?'

I shrugged. 'I'd believe it if I had evidence. So far, I haven't heard any, let alone seen any.'

'Isn't that the trouble, though?' Mairi mused. 'The only way you can really know is…'

'Go for a swim with him?'

She laughed. 'Something like that.'

'I suppose one could always ask him,' I said.

'Oh, no!' Mairi said. 'That would be rude. Anyway, he might not tell the truth.'

'I've never heard of selkies living as humans,' I said. 'Apart from the soldiers, and they were in their own units. So what would a selkie be working on the Skye ferry for?'

'Money?' Mairi laughed.

'He could get a lot more money by strolling in to a biology department, I'll tell you that.'

'Oh?' Mairi looked curious. 'Is it biologists that are interested in them?'

'Well, yes,' I said. 'Who else would be?'

'I don't know. It just seems funny. I don't know about university but I sort of imagined… philosophers or ministers or people like that might be interested.'

'Why them?'

'Well, you know…' She waved a hand. 'Whether selkies have souls and that.'

'Um,' I said. 'I don't know if lecturers in philosophy or divinity would actually need to see a selkie in the flesh, so to speak, before deciding that one way or the other. Scientists, biologists… that's a different story.'

'Yes, I know, but surely the others would at least learn something from *talking* to one.'

I nearly spluttered my Chardonnay, and was about to set Mairi straight on *that*, when her head turned sharply.

'Speak of the devil…'

Cal was standing, his back to us, at the bar. A moment later he turned and saw us. Or rather, he saw me. I felt again that blue electric shock of meeting his gaze. His lips quirked and he nodded casually before turning away to pay for his pint.

I looked back at Mairi. She stared past my shoulder as if hypnotised, then her eyes met mine again.

'OMG OMG!' she said, like a text message. 'He's coming over!'

A moment later Cal stood beside the opposite corner of the table, a full glass in hand, looking down at us and smiling.

'Hello again, Siobhan,' he said. 'Mind if I join you?'

'Oh, no, please, that's fine.'

He sat down facing us.

'Uh, this is Mairi,' I said.

'Hello,' she said.

Cal nodded. 'Pleased to meet you.' He raised his glass. 'Cheers.'

'Cheers!' Mairi and I said.

My heart was hammering. I wondered if Cal had known that we were here. He must have got off work a bit earlier than expected. Maybe he'd dropped by so that my first encounter with him would be in company? But why would he do that? Unless he really was such a scary person that he needed to reassure me? Or did he just come in the Haakon's Arms for a pint after work? If so, why didn't he greet anyone else here? Or…

All sorts of daft thoughts flashed through my mind. Enough.

I took a sip that almost turned into a slurp, put down the glass and said quietly: 'I've heard the word in the village is that you're a selkie.' I said this as if I were sharing a joke.

Cal shot me a straight look, and then his glance flicked sideways to Mairi.

'Yes,' he said. 'That's what they say about me, all right.'

I found myself leaning forward, speaking barely audibly above the background music.

'But is it true?'

Cal leaned back and smiled at me and sipped his pint. 'Would I tell you if it were?'

'You'd better,' I shot back.

'All right,' he said. 'I am.'

Mairi gasped, with a sort of guttural sound in the back of her palate.

'Oh!' I said.

Mairi stuck her face forward, challenging. 'Anybody can *say* that,' she said, apparently forgetting all she'd said about rudeness. 'How could you prove it?'

Cal set his pint to one side. He leaned forward, forearms on the table, palms up. The hands were long, with calluses on the fingertips and across the pads of his thumbs. He spread his fingers. As the digits separated, a glistening, translucent web appeared between them, swiftly thickening to skin, fresh and pink, just like the tiny crescent between the bases of anyone's fingers. He held his hands like that for a few seconds. Then he clenched his fists. When he opened them again, the webbing was gone. He reached for his pint and took a deep gulp.

'Will that do?' he said. 'I can do other wee tricks if you want.' He flicked his thumbnail along his fingernails. 'Claws? They look like mussel shells. I can leave scratches a quarter-inch deep in this table.'

'No, no,' I cried. 'That's enough.'

He looked at Mairi. 'Sure?'

'Oh yes,' she said. Her voice sounded shaky. 'So sometimes the word in the village is true after all, huh?'

'It is that,' said Cal.

'How old are you?' Mairi asked.

I nudged her with my knee under the table. She scowled.

Cal put his brow into the spread of his thumb and forefinger and shook his head slowly in the crook of them, as if he were tired. Then he looked up, smiling.

'Now, now,' he said. 'Is that a polite question?'

'Maybe not,' Mairi admitted. 'Have you always lived here?'

'I come and go,' he said. 'Like the ice.'

He paused for a moment, then laughed at us both. 'Look at your faces! "Like the ice", indeed!'

I smiled, abashed, but a small shiver ran across my shoulders. For a moment there, I'd indeed imagined him coming and going, on a more than millennial itinerary, in alternation with the glaciers' retreat and advance. But that wasn't the source of the shiver. It was the sudden thought that he was laughing at that notion because its scale was *too short.*

Cal swallowed what remained of his pint in one go, put down the empty glass and stood up.

'Well, it's about time I went home,' he said. 'Early start, and all that. See you tomorrow at nine, Siobhan?'

'Yes,' I said. 'At the top of the slipway?'

'That's the place,' he agreed. 'See you there.'

He gazed at me for what was probably only a couple of seconds, then turned for the door. I noticed local lads giving his back a glare as he left. They looked away, as if they didn't want to catch my eye.

'Well!' said Mairi. 'What do you think of that?'

I was quivering inside. 'A bit of a shock,' I said. 'But… you know… he's…'

Mairi laughed. 'If you mean I can see why you fancy him, yes!'

'Um,' I said. '"Fancy" is not quite the right word, actually.'

She put her hand over her mouth and nose, shoulders shaking.

'I can see you got it bad,' she said, after calming down from her fit of the giggles.

She really was quite immature. Her glass was empty. Mine was two-thirds full.

'Fancy another?' I said.

'Yes please,' she said.

At the bar I caught sight of a card of little bags of salted peanuts, and ordered two. I ripped them open as soon as I'd sat down.

'Help yourself,' I said, around a mouthful.

Mairi picked up a single half-peanut and nibbled it like a squirrel.

'I'm watching my weight,' she said, implausibly. 'And you should, too.'

I sipped the dry white wine, which tasted sweet after the

salt.

'I'm not hungry,' I said. 'Just a sudden craving.'

I scooped some more peanuts into my mouth, crunching down, chewing, relishing the rush of salt as I swallowed.

'That's some craving,' said Mairi.

I looked down at two torn sheets of greasy plastic foil. Bits of nut were in awkward corners of my mouth.

'Oh dear,' I said. I took a little wine in my mouth, swilled it around discreetly, and swallowed hard. 'Don't know where that came from.'

Mairi was still looking at me oddly. 'Wherever it came from,' she said, 'maybe it's time we went.'

I'd finished my wine before she'd finished her lager, and was surprised to find that when I stood up I felt unsteadier than she looked. We walked out with some care, ran hand in hand to the end of the road, laughing like crazy, and said goodnight.

'Take care,' Mairi said.

I made my way back to the Crossing Lodge and used my key in the Yale. Light and voices came from the lounge. I crept past and tiptoed upstairs, hearing every creak. In my room I drank a tumbler of water, and decided I must have a shower, late though it was.

Something crunched and jabbed under my bare sole just before I turned the shower off. I yelped, winced, and stooped, water rattling on my shower-cap, to find a clutch of tiny mussel-shells, translucent as a baby's finger-nails.

Four

Starfish, whelks, sea-pinks, sandpipers… these were all depicted on the vinyl apron that Jeanie tossed to me as I stepped into the kitchen the following mid-morning. Likewise apt were the dozen herring and two haddock that she proceeded to show me how to gut, clean, and bone. I had just emerged from the laundry-room with my face hot and my arms aching from an hour or so of ironing. I'd been really looking forward to a cup of tea before my next task, so I joined in the bloody business with ill grace. Jeanie didn't smile, just passed me a pair of disposable plastic gloves and a small sharp knife, and gave me curt instructions as she worked.

'What's the matter?' I said eventually, after she snatched an admittedly mangled fillet from my hands.

'You've messed this one up. It's only good for fishcake now.'

'Sorry,' I said. 'But please tell me, Jeanie. You're upset about something else.'

'You know fine well what it's about!' She deftly extracted a fish head and skeleton from the mush I'd made of the muscle tissue and added it to the stack she was saving for soup. Her lips made a straight line. 'It's you going out with that Cal.'

'I haven't gone out with him,' I said, sliding the tip of the knife's blade behind gill-covers and sawing slowly. 'He just met us in the pub.'

Jeanie gave me a side-long look. 'Where you agreed to meet him tonight. That's a date. Don't try to wriggle out of this, Siobhan.'

'All right,' I said. I slit the ventral side unevenly and began tugging at the organs that spilled out. I didn't bother, or didn't dare, ask Jeanie how she knew. 'I'm not trying to evade it or anything. Cal is a selkie. I'm seeing him for a drink tonight. So what?' I gave her an awkward smile. 'I could be doing it for marine biology, for all you know.'

'A lot *you* know about marine biology,' Jeanie said, 'going by how you cut up fish! Here, give me that.'

She finished the job in seconds, and picked up another fish.

'I'll finish quicker myself,' she said. 'You go and make us a cup of tea.'

I wiped my gloved hands in a bit of kitchen roll, and used the paper to hold the gloves as I took them off and binned them. I went to the sink and wiped down the front of the apron, then filled the kettle and switched it on. Rain was falling heavily enough to set the run-off drumming on the compost-bin lid. The weather forecast had said the rain was here for the day, but that the following two days would be sunny. So we'd have at least a bright Saturday, no doubt followed by a wet Sunday. Great. Sunday was – apart from making beds – a definite day off for me. Jeanie had a lingering sabbatarianism that she didn't take as far as going to church.

Now that Jeanie and I were alone together in the house – all the guests out, and Mairi having left after clearing the breakfast tables – I had a deep dread that I was about to be given an earful of some of Jeanie's other traditional views, as well as her sensible and well-meant advice.

I made a pot of tea, which was ready just as Jeanie finished with the fish. She discarded her gloves, changed aprons, and sat down facing me at the end of the table. She opened a biscuit tin and passed it over as I poured tea.

'Now,' she said, after a few sips and sighs, 'we really need to get this business about Cal sorted out.'

'Uh-huh,' I said, warily.

She sighed again. 'I know you fancy him,' she said, 'and it's very natural in a way, I mean in one sense. Getting people to fall for them, that's *what selkies do*. It's like vampires.'

'They're not a bit like vampires!' I cried. 'They don't *prey* on people!'

'They're like them in that they make people fall for them,' Jeanie said. 'It's in their nature, and it's in ours to fall for the glamour, so in that way it's natural enough, I suppose. But in another way…' She looked away for a moment, then looked back, her face grim. 'In another way it's unnatural, can't you see that?'

'No,' I said. 'I can't.'

'Oh, come on, Siobhan!' she said. 'He's a different *species*, for goodness' sake!'

'He looks human enough to me,' I said. 'More than enough. It can't be unnatural to fancy' – I inwardly winced at the word, it didn't begin to say how I felt – 'a good-looking guy.'

'"A good-looking guy" is an *appearance*. It's something he puts on, like clothes or a mask or – well, no, it's worse than that. It's a whole body he puts on, or takes on. You're an educated girl, Siobhan, I wouldn't be surprised if you've studied something about these creatures. They're not even *animals*. They're not like anything else we know, apart from other sorts of strange beings. Shape-changers.' She shuddered. 'I'm not superstitious, Siobhan, or even very religious as far as that goes, so I don't think they're demonic or anything like that, but they're paranormal, and weird, and dangerous.'

'There are no records of selkies harming people,' I said.

'Not like vampires, we have actual crime statistics for them. And look, Jeanie, I'm only meeting him for a *drink*. Anyway, I can look after myself.'

'Oh, you can, can you?' said Jeanie. 'You'll have taken some "women's self-defence" course at the university, I suppose?'

'Well yes, I have.'

'And you think that would keep you safe from a selkie? He's not like a man, not even a very strong man. These creatures have…' She gazed away until the word came to her. '*Preternatural* strength, that's what they have – and besides, you can't injure them.'

'You can, with electricity,' I said. I was being stubborn, obtuse, and pedantic. I didn't care.

'Well, exactly!' said Jeanie. 'So you're relying on his good will. You can't count on that. You can't even count on fear of punishment. He can just disappear into the sea, any time he wants, and the law can do nothing about it.'

'Yes, it can!' I said, feeling on firmer ground. 'Under the Treaty of St Kilda.'

Jeanie flipped a dismissive hand. 'That's never been tested.'

An oddly technical turn of phrase, I thought.

'And it's never been *tested*,' I said, 'because since then at least, there's never been a charge against a selkie for any crime.'

'Oh, so you know all about that, do you?'

'Well, like you said, I read about them in biology.'

'Yes, I'm sure you did,' said Jeanie. 'But before that, before the treaty, there were plenty of stories about selkies dragging people – women especially – off to sea. Now, I know what you're going to say – that they're just old stories. Well, I'm not an old woman, Siobhan, but I'm old enough to believe some of these old stories. And you would do well to do the same yourself.'

'I'm sorry, Jeanie, but I don't.'

Jeanie sighed. 'Oh well, I'm not your mother. I can't tell

you what to do when you're not at work. But don't bring that creature under my roof.'

'I'd no intention of doing anything of the kind,' I said, indignantly and untruthfully.

'Very well,' said Jeanie. She shrugged. 'You'll do what you will do. I have spoken and saved my soul.'

She said that quite as solemnly as if she'd meant it, then smiled, drained her cup, and brushed biscuit crumbs from the tips of her fingers.

'Time to hoover the stairs,' she said, with nod of her head that made perfectly clear whose job that was. I went off and did it.

As I lugged Mr Sucky the irritatingly cheery vacuum cleaner up from one flight of stairs to another I felt more and more upset. What Jeanie had said seemed a prejudice akin to racism – well, maybe not *that*, given that selkies are a different species or even a different order of being, whatever that means – but it was definitely unjust. It was judging an individual not on his actual behaviour but on his supposed innate characteristics. If he'd been a vampire I could see the point. But surely this was different?

I could feel my righteous indignation draining away. I gave it a boost with the thought that Jeanie was also making a prejudiced judgement on me, as if I'd fallen for some illusion, some glamour – whereas, if she hadn't known Cal was a selkie, she'd have seen from looking at him a very good and natural reason why I might fall for him.

But of course, the same could be said of vampires. There's no doubting their attractive appearance, just from their portraits. I pondered the curious fact that you can't *photograph* vampires, though you can see them, draw them, and paint them. For a moment I found myself thinking particle physics, before I wrenched my mind back to what Jeanie had said.

Anyway, what business was it of hers?

That was my bottom line. I had every right to be angry.

Mr Sucky whined his agreement.

After a hasty and demonstratively talkative lunch break in the kitchen, Jeanie pressed a tenner in my hand and sent me off down the road to the supermarket for two litres of milk, four of various fruit juices, and two bags of sugar. As a scientist, I knew this added up to eight kilograms and was not overjoyed. As a good employee I smiled cheerfully, picked up two heavy-duty shopping bags from their hook behind the kitchen door, and shrugged into my cagoule.

Outside, the air was humid. Rain dripped like sweat from Thor's brow. I hurried along, head down in my hood. It was the smell of tar that made me notice the road-menders. I looked up. A few steps in front of me, a big yellow lorry rolled slowly along by the side of the road. On and around it toiled half a dozen guys in hi-vis waistcoats over tarmac-crusted waterproofs and wellies. One drove, two signalled to traffic, two shovelled and smoothed the tarry chips that slithered from its tipper, and one a few metres behind pushed a heavy roller to tamp it all down.

The roller-pusher looked up. His face broke into a broad grin. My own mouth must have gaped.

The man was Kieran, my ex. For a moment I hadn't recognised him – in the weeks since I'd last seen him, his previously unruly red-brown hair had been given a modish cut, and he'd grown a neatly razor-trimmed jaw-line beard to match. His face had acquired enough tan to merge his freckles.

'Well hello, Siobhan,' he said, pausing and leaning on the two big handles of the roller. 'What are you doing here?'

There was a note of surprise in his voice, but it rang false. I'd got to know him too well in our two months together.

'I'm working for the summer,' I said. 'What are you doing?'

'The same.' He waved vaguely at the truck, and resumed his forward plod. I glanced over my shoulder and skipped a few steps back to keep pace.

'Why here, though?' I asked. 'There are plenty of summer jobs in Glasgow, and you'd be close to Julia –'

Kieran flinched slightly. An awful thought struck me. 'Is *Julia* here too?'

Another flinch. His face reddened. 'Uh, no, we, uh… It didn't work out. It was a mistake in the first place, and I realised –'

The situation snapped into focus.

'Don't you *dare* say it!' I said. 'Just. Fucking. Don't.'

'I know I should have said that to you before now, but –'

'So you thought you'd follow me here?'

'No, no… I have relatives in Portree, and –'

'You're telling me you *didn't know* I was here?'

He let go of the handles, and spread his hands. 'How could I know?' The handles swayed forward and he grabbed them, favouring me with a sheepish grin. I responded with a glare.

'I can think of a few ways,' I said. 'And I'm not hearing you deny it. You can't deny it, can you?'

Kieran glanced sideways.

'Well, not exactly, but it's not like I'm stalking you, just –'

At this point all my anger at Jeanie's aspersions boiled over to scald Kieran. I gave him a piece of my mind at the top of my voice and strode off down the road, shaking with self-righteousness.

Five

On the west coast of Scotland weather doesn't just happen: it arrives. You can see it coming, usually marching in off the Atlantic. In Kyleakin the rain rolls down off the Cuillins and the wind funnels up the Inner Sound. The humidity and drizzle of the afternoon had by 9 p.m. combined with a stiff breeze to form what is fondly known in Scotland as 'a wetting rain'. I stood at the top of the slipway and shivered under my cagoule and sweater. My skinny jeans were already soaked. Through cloud cover the midsummer sun glimmered feebly and (as it seemed to me) too high in the sky.

'Well, hello,' said Cal, looming out of the drizzle.

He was wearing polished shoes, clean jeans and a check shirt with the sleeves rolled up. This must be his idea of dressing for a date. I could see droplets on the tips of his arm hairs but his clothes looked bone dry. He might have just stepped out of an air-conditioned car.

'Hello,' I said.

'So here we are,' he said, in a wondering voice. 'Where would you like to go?'

'Somewhere dry and warm?'

'The Old Castle's the nearest place.'

What Mairi had told me about the Old Castle – empty but

for grumpy old men – didn't appeal, but I was in no mood to quibble.

'Sounds like a plan,' I said.

We set off briskly, side by side, Cal keeping his awkward distance as if we just happened to be walking in parallel.

'You must have got off early?' I said, making conversation.

'How?'

'You've had time to change.'

'Yes, that I have,' said Cal, sounding amused.

I didn't inquire further, because the thought that struck me almost made me stumble. Of course he'd had *time to change*...

Or was that a crazy thought? Did his shape-shifting ability go no further than his skin?

And then, of course, I thought about his skin. The tiny glittering beads on the hairs of his arms. I stole a sideways glance and felt a quiver inside. Distracted, I stumbled on a wet cobble. Cal's hand shot out to grip my forearm. Steadied, but jolted: I twitched. He let go.

The Old Castle had a faded depiction of the ruined castle on its signboard, and an old guy standing beside the doorway contemplating the smoke from his pipe and ignoring the rain dripping from the peak of his cap. He may have spared Cal a nod as we went in.

Inside, the pub was quite different from what Mairi had led me to expect. The front room was the domain of a dozen or more young people, none of whom I recognised and most, going by their accents, students on summer jobs. It would have been just my luck if Kieran had been there, but to my relief he wasn't. The music was chart pop-rock and loud. Evidently the pub's strategy was to draw new customers by alienating its regulars. In the back room, up a step like a stage, the remaining five or six grumpy old men huddled around one table, playing dominoes. I noticed several hearing-aids on the table: a good way of tuning out the music.

'What'll you have?'

I was suddenly thirsty, or my mouth was dry.

'A pint of… something local?'

Cal appraised me and the pump handles in one sweeping glance.

'Skye Light,' he prescribed. 'Can't get more local than that.'

He eyed corners, spotted a vacancy, indicated, all in another smooth flow of the gaze.

'Grab a seat. With you in a minute.'

I hastened to a table in a corner of the back room. The old men's conversation, which I could have sworn I'd been half-overhearing in English, paused for a beat and resumed in Gaelic. I swept the geezers a fixed grin and made for the corner table. Cal, I guessed, would prefer to sit with his back to the wall. I took the chair rather than the bench and hung my cagoule over the seat-back. A surprise as I sat down: my jeans were dry. The cagoule still dripped.

Cal arrived with a brace of glasses and bottles. His was Red Cuillin, a darker brew than mine. He poured deftly and set the drinks down, then himself.

'Cheers.'

'Cheers.'

Again the blue shock of meeting his eyes. I could have just… I don't know. But it seemed important to maintain my composure. To keep my head above water.

Water.

'My knees were soaked,' I said. 'Now they're dry.'

'Interesting,' said Cal.

'Was that you?'

He shrugged and sighed. 'It could have been. I don't know. I don't fully control the phenomena, you understand.'

'I don't understand!'

He closed his eyes for a moment. 'A lot of people seem to think' – he rapped the knuckles of both fists on his sternum –

'there's a selkie in *here*, wearing *this*' – the spread fingers of both hands passed down in front of his face – 'like a mask. That the selkie is the real self, and the human form is an avatar.' He frowned. 'Like in a computer game, you know?'

'I know,' I said. 'And yes, a lot of people do think exactly that.'

'Well, it's not,' he said. 'It's more like there's me, Cal, and then there's this other thing I'm part of.'

'How do you mean, part of?'

'If I could put it into words, I would. It's hard to explain. I don't just look like a human being. I feel like one, all the way through, just one that can do things other people can't. Yet I also know fine well I'm not.' He laughed, with a dismissive gesture. 'Most of the time, I don't even think about it.'

'What memories do you have?'

'You're a great one for the tact,' Cal said lightly. He must have read my dismayed look – my directness was just the sort of thing Kieran had complained about – because he hastily added: 'Sorry, I didn't mean it like that. But to answer what I think is your question – I have no memories of a human childhood, or adolescence.' He shrugged. 'All I can remember is being me as I am.'

'Mairi said you turned up two years ago,' I said. 'What were you doing before that?'

'I was in the sea.'

He said it with a flat finality that didn't invite questions.

'And before that? The last time you were human?'

He gave me a twitch of a smile. 'Och, much the same. I was always on the boats, one way or another. It was easier back before forms and qualifications and easier yet when most people couldn't read or write.'

I stared at him, feeling again that glacial chill, that cold current.

'How far back is that? What, *centuries*?'

Cal spread his hands. 'How should I know? Before the nineteenth, well… I heard mention of the fourth year of James, and the like.' He smiled reminiscently. 'There have been a lot of Jameses in Scotland, and two in England. I mind times when folk never mentioned what year of our Lord it was, never mind what century.'

At that I heard over my right shoulder 'Calum Mack!' followed by a harsh loud sentence in Gaelic that cut across the ambient music and conversation like a claymore through cobwebs. Cal's gaze flicked fractionally to the left and up. I turned sharply.

One of the old men at the table across the way had just returned from a smoke – his tweed jacket and check shirt reeked of it, and there was ash on his tie. He stood by his vacant seat glaring at Cal. He said something quieter, in Gaelic, leaning with one hand on the back of his seat, as if awaiting a response.

Cal narrowed his eyes and nodded once. 'Okay, okay. I meant no offence.'

'What's this about?' I asked.

'The lady does not have the Gaelic,' Cal explained, as if this needed pointing out.

The old man switched his attention to me. 'I was reminding your friend here,' he said, 'that the name of our Lord should not be on his lips. Not even as a figure of speech.'

I rocked back a little. 'What? Why ever not?'

The old man held out a hand towards me and swept it around, as if to encompass me and his cronies and the youngsters in the other room in the same gesture, then pointed at Cal.

'*Our* Lord,' he said, 'is not *his* Lord.'

This struck me as theologically dubious. It didn't seem the moment to raise that point.

'And who would Cal's Lord be?' I demanded.

'If you stick around with that one you'll find out soon enough,' the old man told me, with a dark chuckle.

'What do you mean?'

'You'll lose your life,' he said. 'And you'll lose your soul.'

'Oh yes?' I gave him a cold look. 'Whereas drinking, smoking and dominoes are the way to heaven, are they?'

'You won't find a word in the Book against them,' the man said. 'Whereas you will find plenty of warnings against consorting with unclean spirits.'

I closed my eyes and shook my head. I couldn't think what to say to that – well, I could think of a lot of things to say, most of which would get me thrown out of the pub.

'I don't believe I'm doing any such thing,' I said. 'And I don't believe in spirits, or in your Book for that matter. I'm a scientist.'

This last was not strictly true.

'Oh, it's a scientist you are? And there was me thinking you were just a foolish lassie.'

'Now hold it there, Uilleam,' said Cal. 'That is getting personal.'

'My apologies, miss,' the man said.

'I don't think it's me you insulted,' I said.

'Oh, it was. Insult Calum? Ha! It's water off a duck's back to that one. So to speak!'

A knowing elderly laugh echoed around the table.

Cal, to my surprise, guffawed. 'He's right there!'

'What would be polite,' I said, 'would be to mind your own business.'

The old man huffed, taken aback.

'Well, I have no wish to argue. The doors of salvation are open for you, if not for him.'

And with that he turned back to his dram and his dominoes.

I looked at Cal and mouthed: *What the fuck?*

Cal supped his pint and returned me a level gaze.

'Do you want to leave?'

'No,' I said. 'I won't give the bigots that satisfaction.'

'Ach, they're no bigots,' Cal said. 'The *bodach* meant well, in his way. And I did forget myself, using that expression.'

'You seem very slow to take offence.'

'I challenged him when he called you names,' Cal pointed out. 'As for me, well, I've heard worse.'

'And taken it?'

'Oh yes. What else am I to do? My kind may live for… a long time, by your reckoning, but we're not immortal. We can be killed. And we can kill, but… the numbers are not in our favour. In another time, what I said without thinking could have got me burned to ashes, doubtless not before I had done such damage as would have made the sentence seem just. Even these days… I have no intention of rising to any bait, put it that way.'

Civil though it had been, Uilleam's unforgiving, unflinching certainty had unsettled me. I put my hands to the sides of my face, and spoke quietly.

'Was there any truth in what he said?'

Cal gave me a guarded look. 'In what way?'

'Do you… Do the selkies have, or think they have… another, uh, Lord?'

'No,' said Cal. 'The selkies serve no master, in this world or any other. And if this world has a ruler, we know nothing of such a being.'

'That's a relief,' I said, a little shakily. 'Well, I don't either. And I'm not sure I want to.'

'A wise precaution,' said Cal. 'Whether such a highest one

exists or not, it seems best not to pry into its intentions or trifle with its affairs.'

I had to laugh. 'What a shame that opinion is not more widely shared!'

Cal took my point more specifically than I'd intended.

'Yes,' he said, 'it's a pity about the vampires all right.'

'What?'

'It's all true about them,' he said gloomily. 'They really do worship, most of them anyway, and their object of devotion really is the personage yon *bodach* was hinting was mine.'

'Old Nick?'

'The very same.' He sighed. 'But what else can you expect of the poor suckers, coming from that place beyond the dark forest where they were beset by peasant Unitarians? I've tried disputing the matter with a vampire or two in my time, and I wouldn't recommend it.'

'I've no intention of trying, I assure you,' I said. I knocked back the rest of my pint. 'Same again?'

As I waited at the bar I found myself struck by how odd it was that on our first date – as I definitely thought of it, whatever I'd said to Jeanie – we'd found ourselves talking about the religion of vampires, of all things, and not sport, politics, telly, gossip, or whatever it is normal people talk about on first dates.

My notion of normal people, of course, was a bit skewed by –

'Five-fifty,' said the barman.

I handed over the note and the coin, picked up the beers, turned –

To see Kieran emerge from the Gents'. He acknowledged

me with a nod and a half-smile, as if to say *let's pretend we didn't see each other.* Now that he was wearing a short-sleeved shirt rather than oilskins, I could see how his arm muscles had bulked up from a fortnight of pushing the tarmac-roller and suchlike healthy exercise in the open air. Even his posture was more confident than I remembered from term-time. He recovered a half-sunk pint from a shelf beside a small group of likewise strapping lads he'd evidently been drinking with, and strolled into the back room like a man without a care in the world.

I recovered my composure and hurried after him. Maybe one of the *bodaich* was a relative of his or something.

But no.

'Excuse me,' I heard him say to Cal.

'Yes?'

'Hi, my name's Kieran. Do you mind if I ask you a few questions?'

Cal, with an apologetic glance at me, motioned him to sit down. That he did, in the seat beside mine. I went over, planted the pints, and sat down. Kieran looked at me, surprised – genuinely this time, I had to admit – and then smiled.

'Great minds think alike, I see,' he said. 'Hope you don't mind.'

'What?' I said. 'What alike?'

'You're doing marine biology next year too, aren't you?'

I closed my eyes and opened them again. 'What do you mean, "too"?'

'I signed up for a course next semester,' said Kieran. 'Anyway…'

Oblivious to my no doubt gob-smacked look, he turned his attention back to Cal. 'I'm sure Siobhan here has asked you all this already, so, you know, excuse me if I'm boring you and all that, but I was wondering if you or any of your, uh, people might be willing to share any information you might have of, say, sea life around the northwest coast of Scotland and that?'

Cal leaned back and looked from Kieran to me. 'Do you know each other?'

Kieran snorted. 'You could say that.'

I glared at him, and said to Cal: 'He's my ex. That's to say, he dumped me a few months ago.'

'Ah,' said Cal, as if baffled but processing the concept. 'No, Siobhan hasn't asked me any such questions. I was about to ask her why she had called herself a scientist, and now it seems you have answered that.'

I felt suddenly flustered and defensive, on top of being furious with Kieran. 'When I said that… it was a slight exaggeration. I'm a student, and I'm thinking of switching to a science degree course.'

'And studying marine biology?'

'Yes,' I said. 'Or I *was*, before Kieran put his oar in.'

'What do you mean?' Kieran asked.

I restrained the impulse to grab him by the shirt-front and shake him. 'I'm interested in marine biology anyway, but what really pushed me to study it next year was because I wanted to get away from *you*. But now it looks like you've followed me there too.'

'That's not true!' Kieran said. 'Jeez, Siobhan, I wish you would drop this idea that I'm following you around.'

'You're telling me,' I said, 'that it's *pure coincidence* that you've got work in the very same village as me, that you signed up to the same course next year as I did, and that now you're right here in the very same pub where I and Cal have gone for a drink?'

'You and Cal?' I could see the light dawning. 'You mean you're *going out* with him?'

He sounded incredulous and amused.

'Yes! Well, I hope I am.'

I turned to Cal for confirmation and support, and was dismayed to meet his frown.

'You didn't tell me about your interest in marine biology,' he said.

'I was going to,' I said. 'Like you said, you were about to ask, and I'd have answered just as I did a moment ago.'

'Yes,' he said. 'And I would have been just as concerned as I am now.'

'Concerned? Why?'

'Well,' he said, spreading his hands, 'you must know that my kind have some experience with marine biologists. We don't exactly *share knowledge* with them, Kieran. We aren't the researchers. We're the ones that get *researched on*.'

'I didn't –' Kieran began.

'So you'll excuse me. Siobhan, Kieran.'

With that Cal stood up, drank his fresh pint in one go, nodded, and went out. He was through the door before I could grab up my cagoule and bag. Pausing only to snarl, 'You bloody idiot!' at Kieran, I rushed out and looked up and down the road. The clouds had cleared and the east was blue and starry. Cal was already fifty metres away, walking with brisk strides.

I ran after him. He must have heard my pelting feet, but he didn't look back. He turned around the shoulder of a tall house. I reached it moments later. There was no sign of him. In a distant backyard a dog barked, and something else growled back at it.

There was still light in the sky. I walked back to the Crossing Lodge, and only my face got wet on the way.

'I told you,' said Mairi, with gloomy relish. 'There's many a one has tried, but no one has got off with that one.'

We were on our first break of the morning, and she and Gordon had nipped out the back for a smoke. I joined them to breathe fresh air and watch the little gang of sparrows around the bird feeder. I wanted to talk about what had happened, and not with Jeanie. Jeanie had tactfully said nothing, though she had glanced up from a stint of late-evening tapestry with a quirk of eyebrow at my unexpectedly early return.

'It wasn't like that,' I said. 'It was all just a misunderstanding.'

Gordon shook his head. 'They're both being dicks about it.'

I laughed, startled out of my anguished retreading of the previous evening's events by this unexpected perspective. Yes, when you looked at it that way…

'Yes!' I said. 'It's their problem.'

I decided, then and there, that I was not going to let my ex or my intended put me off the study of the life of the sea. I'd always enjoyed swimming. I'd always been fascinated by rock pools and all the tiny hardscrabble lives within. I'd read books about sharks and whales and watched documentaries about the alien intelligence of octopuses. I'd joined the university's Sub-Aqua Club right at the Freshers' Fair, and been an enthusiastic participant in its weekend expeditions. If Kieran was going to be doing marine biology as his science option when we went back to university in September, I would just have to thole it. And if Cal found my interest suspect, why then I would just have to thole that.

'I don't get it,' Mairi said.

'Don't worry,' I said. 'I'm fine.'

I wasn't, really, but I went back to work in a much more cheerful mood.

Six

That Sunday, the weather – confirming the weather forecast, though not my glum foreboding – stayed sunny. I had most of the day off, and no one to spend it with. After making the beds, I grabbed a ham roll and water bottle from the kitchen and sloped off to my own bedroom and packed them in a rucksack with my *Collins Pocket Guide to the Sea Shore* and a notebook. After a minute's pondering my dry-suit in front of the open wardrobe, I decided that it was too bulky for a casual carry and anyway what I really wanted was sea on my skin – however briefly, however cold. I hastily changed so that I had a swimsuit on under my T-shirt and jeans, and stuffed my underwear in at the bottom of the rucksack, then my mask, snorkel and flippers, with a swim-cap, a towel and sun-cream on top of the lot. It added up to quite a load and the flippers stuck out of the top.

Feeling self-conscious, I left the Lodge – to a wry glance from Jeanie – and set off for the shore. I turned off the main road, across the little inlet behind the part of the village on the approach to the slipway, and up towards the ruined castle. This stretch of sea was where the submarine had run aground. The shoal of its stranding was now marked by a small red buoy. Across the water I could see a couple of islets, part of Kyle of

Lochalsh with its snaking queue of vehicles, and the Balmacara woods and hills beyond. Sailing dinghies leaned, lobster-boats crawled, and the two ferries plied. With a sudden pang, I wondered if Cal was aboard one of them, and if he was thinking of me.

Of course I'd heard nothing from him. The days after Keiran's break-up with me had been punctuated by wary text messages, stiff mutual assurances. I'd never thought to ask for Cal's phone number, and he'd never asked for mine: for all I knew, he didn't even have a phone.

I struck out across the scrubby headland and at a convenient and promising cove scrambled down to the rocky shore. The beach was steeply sloped. I crunched and slithered over pebbles and sat down on a gnarly outcrop close to the water. The sea was calm. Nobody was around. A cormorant raced its reflection across the water. The only sounds were the gulls above, the bees working the heather and gorse behind me, the hiss of the breaking waves, and the fizz of barnacles opening to welcome the salty splash of the incoming tide. The smells of the heather and gorse mingled with those of fresh seaweed.

I consulted my handbook and peered at the tiny shells that encrusted the lower part of the rock I was sitting on. Ah yes, *Balanus balanoides*, just as I'd expected. I went back up the little beach and found a dry hollow under a tussock of heather. I took the flippers and mask and snorkel out of the bag, and stuffed my outer clothes in. I religiously slapped water-resistant sun cream on my shoulders, arms and legs, and tied back my hair and pulled on the swim-cap. Then I picked my way down to the water, wincing at the occasional sharp stone or broken shell on my bare soles. As I waded in clutching my gear I felt the pebbles underfoot become rounder and bigger.

Knee-deep, and my teeth chattered. This early in the summer, the sea hadn't had time to store much heat. It was, in short, bloody cold. But I'd expected this, and stoically waded in a bit deeper, then crooked my knees and plunged forward. After that first shock I stood up, now waist-deep and no longer shivering. I slipped the snorkel through its rubber loop on the mask's tie, and awkwardly squirmed the flippers and mask on. This took more than one attempt: sand in the flippers, condensation in the mask. But eventually I got everything snug and clear.

A quick glance around to confirm my orientation, then I gripped the snorkel behind my lips and ducked into the water. Snorkelling makes swimming a different, less fraught, experience. Once you get the hang of the occasional stops and starts imposed by the ping-pong ball valve, breathing becomes something you don't have to think about, and you feel more like you're floating or flying than swimming. With a few thrusts of my flippers I was past the bladder-wrack and above the long waving fronds of *Laminaria.* For a minute or two I drifted, spotting sea-anemones and cold-water soft corals, and little darting fish. The sunlight, refracted by water and the Perspex of my mask, seemed to radiate outward from the centre of my visual field in great spokes.

I blew water out of the snorkel, took a few deep breaths, and dived. My ears popped and I swallowed hard. I was now beyond the seaweed forest and the sea-floor was rocky with patches of sand, on which the odd bit of litter – aluminium cans, rusted iron debris – stood out. Crabs ambled, fish darted or hovered, fanning their pectoral fins, and shrimp stirred the sand with the feathery frenzy of their whirring legs. Here and there I could see the loose sandy worm-casts of razor-clams.

I returned to the surface, and spat out the snorkel mouthpiece to gasp. A sudden swell, probably the wake of a ship far out of sight, bobbed me up and down a few times. I trod water effortlessly with my flippers, and pushed up my mask to take advantage of the water's rise and fall to look around. By now I was about thirty metres from the beach. It was still empty, and no gulls or crows had discovered my rucksack.

Seaward, I saw a flash and a splash, then another. At first I thought they were intersecting wakes, but soon recognised what was going on. A few hundred metres out, a pod of porpoises sported. I let the wave lift me again and again, and gazed with delight at the lithe, leaping black shapes. And then they were gone.

Ten minutes in the sea and the cold was beginning to get to me. I turned around and struck out for shore. As I reached the shallower water the seaweed began to brush my legs. The sensation was familiar, and not unpleasant. Then it seemed a frond got wrapped around my ankle. I shook my foot, and the clammy grip tightened. Alarmed, I jack-knifed around, and in a flurry of splashes stood up in waist-deep water.

Whatever had caught my ankle let go. That was what it felt like, a willed release, not a slipping off. Then, just two metres from me, the sea erupted. For a moment it was as if one of the porpoises I'd seen offshore had leaped up vertically in front of me. That was what I thought I saw, before the first blink. Then it was as if the sea itself rose up, towering above me. It seemed to hang there, poised for a moment, and then several cubic metres of water came down with a mighty splash.

The surge sent me staggering and flailing. I landed on my buttocks on a clump of weed. By the time I'd struggled to my flipper-clad feet the surge had diminished to ripples, and where it had come from stood a naked man, in water up to his thighs. The fair hair that hung thick to his shoulders had not a drop of water on it; nor, as far as I can remember, did his chest and arms. I pushed up my mask and stared at him in terror and awe.

Cal was handsome; Cal was good-looking; Cal had stolen my heart with a glance. This selkie was beautiful, like a Norse god imagined by a Greek sculptor. Or, to go from the sublime to the ridiculous, he looked as I'd imagined He-Man would look like in real life (so to speak) when I'd played with his action figure or watched the cartoons when I was six years old. Well, like He-Man would have looked if his hair had been longer and if he'd been bollock naked. You might think a selkie manifesting in human form to a lone woman on a beach might decently drape his hips with seaweed. This one didn't.

Terrified though I was, I had enough presence of mind to know what I faced. This was a selkie with glamour turned to the max. The sun was hot on my shoulders, the drips from stray strands of hair cold down my back.

'Who are you?' the selkie said. His voice was deep and mellow, his accent cultured.

I tried to recall if it was dangerous to tell a selkie your name. Nothing in the science, and nothing even in the stories… It seemed selkies weren't among the actively predatory but oddly legalistic Metamorpha such as vampires. (I'm fairly sure that spells and bindings and so forth are simply reminders of legal requirements, like reading a suspect their rights.) But the science and the stories agreed that selkies could be insistent, and irresistible.

'My name's Siobhan,' I said, backing away slowly. 'Who are you?'

'My name,' said the selkie, 'is unpronounceable in air. It has a fine ring to it underwater.' He smiled slyly. 'Do you wish to hear it spoken there?'

'No!' I said, alarmed by the sudden sway I felt towards the insinuating invitation. 'I'm a human being and a British subject and I claim the protection of the Treaty of St Kilda.'

'So do I,' said the selkie, in a tone of grave amusement, like a grandfather indulging a toddler. 'It is of the Treaty I would speak. Your kind are testing it severely.'

'How?' I asked.

'The submarines,' he said, jerking a thumb over his shoulder in a disarmingly human manner.

'Oh!' I said. 'Like the one that ran aground out there.'

'It did not run aground accidentally,' said the selkie. 'The shoal it stranded on was not on the charts because it had not previously been there.'

'Oh!' I said again. 'You mean selkies made it?'

'I did not say that.' The selkie's smile was sly. 'But we have a difficulty with the submarines. A treaty violation. They have been encroaching on the following areas –'

'Stop!' I waved both hands in front of my face. 'You can't tell me that! Where submarines go is top secret, it's a national security question. I could be in deep trouble if I was told that. Besides, I'm not the person to talk to. I have no authority or standing in the matter. You have to take this up with the Navy or the Admiralty or, uh, HM Coastguard or whatever.'

'No,' said the selkie. A frown creased his broad brow. 'I cannot do that, and nor can those of us who object to the encroachments. Those of us who speak with the Navy do not object to them.'

I was flummoxed. 'You have… spokespersons? And not all selkies agree with them?'

'That is not quite how it is,' said the selkie. 'It would be complicated to explain.' He shrugged and spread his hands. 'To come to agreements requires an affinity on both sides, and on both sides it is rare. That is why I am talking to you.'

'But I don't –'

'But you do,' said the selkie. 'You have known us since you were small.' He smiled. 'Do you not remember?'

I remembered, all right. 'Was that you?'

The selkie nodded. I didn't recall the one I'd encountered in the sea off Millport as being quite as striking in appearance as this one, but then of course selkies are shape-shifters, and –

At that point a shocking thought struck me.

'Are you Cal?'

The selkie gazed at me impassively.

'No,' said a voice behind me.

I looked over my shoulder, to see Cal standing a few metres up the beach. Before I had time to react, a huge splash drenched me all over again. I turned back just in time to see a black streamlined shape under the water, and a V-shaped wake arrowing away.

'Well, thanks for that,' I said to the indifferent sea. Then I turned around and tramped back up the shingle. In the last shallow surf I took the flippers off.

'I'll talk to you in a minute,' I said to Cal as I picked my way past him in bare feet.

'I'll wait,' he said.

Cal sat on a boulder staring out to sea while I dried myself and changed. Properly shod again, I traipsed across the beach and faced Cal. He sat with his elbows on his knees. He was wearing double denim and a rock-band T-shirt and his old scuffed trainers. Somehow he carried it off, or maybe that was the glamour.

'Did you follow me here?' I asked, in an accusing tone.

'No,' he said. 'I was drawn here by the selkie, as were you.'

'Oh come *on*,' I said. 'You can't expect me to believe in *telepathy*!'

'You've just seen something much more remarkable than telepathy,' Cal pointed out wryly. 'But no, I don't expect you to believe in it. I don't think telepathy's involved, anyway.' He scuffed moodily at the shingle. 'The summoning signal may be sub-sonic.'

'Well, I didn't come here to see a selkie, and I didn't hear any signal.'

'You don't hear it,' said Cal. 'That's the point. So why did you come here?'

'To do a wee bit of elementary marine biology, just to annoy you.'

He raised his eyebrows. 'To annoy me? Really?' He sounded pleased.

'Yes, and because… I wanted to go in the sea.'

'You wanted to go in the sea,' said Cal, nodding as if to himself. 'Summoned.'

'I wasn't summoned.'

'You're here,' he pointed out. 'What would you call it?'

'In any case,' I said, slightly annoyed by his smugness, 'if it was something sub-sonic then the submarines' sonar and all the ship engine noises would – oh!'

'And yon's the problem,' said Cal. He stood up. 'May I take you for a drive?'

We walked back, across the headland behind the castle and over the little creek to the main road, not saying much along the way. His car was a very ordinary white Mazda, but he seemed inordinately proud of it. It smelled of polymers and esters. A pine air freshener dangled from the mirror. He took me for a drive and talked about steam.

'Steam engines were the first,' said Cal. He dawdled past the tail-end of the Sunday ferry queue, then pressed down hard on the gas pedal, high-tailing it out of Kyleakin. 'And the worst we'd faced up to then. Before that, there were nets, sometimes harpoons. But they were accidental, most of the time. And on the land there was the persecution of superstition.' He laughed abruptly. 'Most of us would prefer a superstitious fear over a scientific curiosity, any day! But as I was saying… sail and oars, we could live with that. For thousands of years we had lived with that. There was nothing in their sound that differed much from the wind and the waves. And then it started – the terrible throb. It took us a while to figure it out. The first to hear that throb thought it was earthquakes, or underwater landslides rumbling off the continental shelf. Then they made the connection with the new fast ships, with their thrashing paddles.'

We were passing along a dull stretch of the A850: *machair* to the right, moorland to the left. Tussocks and erosion gullies and old tractor tyres, each with their own whirlwind of midges. But across the sound to the north the mountains of Torridon shouldered the clouds, and ahead the Cuillin loomed. Amid that banality, and against that antiquity, Cal's bantering reminiscent tone about a time before my great-great-grandmother was born seemed quite in order.

'Then came the propellers and the diesel engines and sonar pings and undersea cables and all the rest, a huge build-up of shipping, and the noise – not just sound, mind you, but electro-magnetic – was getting worse all the time. The Treaty gave us some respite – there are more marine conservation areas than you'll find on any map – but it's getting frayed. Especially here around the islands, all the way up the west coast and around to the northern isles. Offshore wind-farms and undersea turbines are here, more are coming, and with them yet more annoyances.'

'But weren't selkies involved in the Second World War?' I said. 'And more must have been in military operations since. Surely that means selkies can tolerate noise.'

'Some can,' Cal said in a grim tone. 'We're as different in what we can tolerate as you are. And as different in our opinions. Those who can put up with a lot of noise tend to be the same ones as work with the military. And those who can't, or won't, tend to be those who don't. And they don't have the ear of the Admiralty. As far as the government is concerned, those who do are our leaders and representatives.'

'What about scientists and conservationists and so on?' I said. 'Surely they –'

I stopped. When someone's telling you a problem you know nothing about, it's never a good idea to start a reply with 'Surely'.

'Well, no,' said Cal, mildly in the circumstances. 'The scientists still see us as interesting objects of study, like some kind of strange beast, and the conservationists see us as a menace to the kind of marine life they want to protect: fish stocks, seals, marine mammals and so on. To them, we're something like pollution or an invasive predator species.'

'And are you?'

Cal chuckled darkly, keeping his gaze on the road. 'Well, that's a bold and honest question, and it deserves a like answer. The truth is, Siobhan, I don't know. There are not enough of us to affect fish stocks, and we take the odd seal and maybe bigger prey here and there. But we are invasive and alien, in that we came from elsewhere –'

'Where?'

'That I don't know.' He smiled. 'A bit before my time. There are myths, but they're sung, and like yon selkie's name they only make sense underwater. Like the songs of the great whales. They're not in words in the first place. And they're hard to put into words when you're out of the sea. You know the experience of not remembering a dream, and the more you try the more you forget?'

'Yes,' I said.

'I don't,' said Cal. 'But I'm told your people do, and I think that's what it's like. Anyway – we're from outside the Earth, we eat plenty and nothing eats us, so perhaps over the long term we do upset the balance of nature, or whatever they call it these days. How would I know? I'm not a marine biologist.' He glanced sidelong at me. 'Was that the sort of thing you were wanting to find out?'

'No!' I cried. 'It never crossed my mind. If you'd given me a chance to explain, after that idiot ex-boyfriend of mine…'

I sniffed hard, and said nothing for long enough to notice.

'Yes?' he said.

I hesitated, as if on a high board, then took the plunge. 'You've got this all wrong. I don't want to research on you, it's not about that. It's got nothing to do with marine biology.'

'What has got nothing to do with it?'

My mouth was suddenly dry, my palms damp.

'What I feel about you,' I said.

The muscle at the angle of his jaw stood out. His knuckle whitened on the wheel.

'Oh,' he said. 'The glamour got you. I'm sorry about that, Siobhan. I did not mean for that to happen.'

He sounded so apologetic I almost felt sorry for him. Then I felt angry.

'But how do *you* feel?'

'About you?'

'Yes, about me!'

He kept his gaze on the road.

'The glamour works on us both,' he said. 'I fell for you as you fell for me, Siobhan.'

My heart lurched.

'Why me, and not all the other girls who –'

'I could flatter you about that, and there would be some truth in it' – he smiled sidelong –' but the real truth is that none of them had the affinity. And as I just heard the other selkie tell you, you do. I felt it the moment I saw you on the ferry, across that car roof in the rain.'

He slowed the car as we entered Broadford, passing the nuclear power station on the shore. 'But I can't act on how I feel.'

'Why not?' I cried. 'If we both feel the same way, why not?'

'Because the glamour cares nothing for our happiness, and I do. And besides' – he risked another sideways glance, and his voice became more cheerful – 'you and I, we have something far more important to do.'

I could have killed him. He was driving, and past a hospital at that, so I didn't.

We stopped in Portree for lunch. Cal parked the car and took me to a pub by the main square where, he said, they did very good fish and chips. I looked askance as he ordered pints for both of us while we waited.

'Drinking and driving?'

Cal smiled. 'Metabolism varies.'

'Oh.'

Cal scanned the crowded bar and made a bee-line for the one vacant small table. The surrounding hubbub gave us privacy to talk.

'So what,' I said, mutinously, 'is this *far more important* thing we have to do?'

Cal leaned forward, our foreheads almost touching. It was like being inches from a Van de Graaf generator. I felt as if at any moment my hair would spring into a mad-scientist frizz.

'We have to find someone to talk to, someone in authority, and bring the concerns I mentioned to their attention. I could not do that on my own, because… Well, I would have no idea how to go about it. And you could not, on your own, because why should anyone listen?'

'What do you mean, you have no idea? You read books, don't you?'

'Only old ones. But yes, I could look it all up in a library, I suppose.'

'Or online?'

He shook his head. 'We don't have a good relationship with electricity,' he said. 'In either direction, you could say.' He looked grim for a moment, and I recalled the old pictures of rubber troughs and Faraday cages. 'Electronics is worse. On the old phones, the interference was there, but you could hear and speak above the crackling. If I use a phone now, the battery dies in my hand before I can finish entering the number. I can drive all right, as you know, but the car radio or the CD player – forget it. And if I sit down in front of a computer, the screen goes to snow. But even if I read all about the institutions on paper, I would have a problem approaching the authorities. I don't have the right documents.'

'You must have something,' I said. 'You're employed. You must have paperwork.'

Cal leaned back, and rubbed the nape of his neck.

'Um,' he said. 'I have a union card.' He fingered a laminated RMT card from his shirt pocket, and flourished it under my nose before slipping it back. 'That's it. I'm not officially on the payroll. I get paid the going rate, but in cash, and it's listed under incidental expenses, running costs like diesel and so on. How can a company legally employ someone with no ID? I don't have so much as a birth certificate, let alone a passport or a bank account.'

'So, wait, you're saying you're employed illegally?'

'I am not saying that at all,' said Cal, sounding affronted. 'All shipping companies, and the Navy for that matter, have like arrangements. It's all square with the Revenue, too.'

'But why?'

'Well now,' he said, 'if we were on the books we'd need some kind of official recognition beyond the Treaty, and that's a can that all concerned are happy to kick down the road.'

'So why don't your people tackle it from the other side?' I said. 'Like, you said the ones who work with the Admiralty are taken as representatives. Surely' – there I went again, but I ploughed on – 'you could *change* those representatives?'

Cal laughed, and took a deep swig of his pint.

'It's not a democracy,' he said. 'It's not even a kingdom.' He leaned closer, beery-breathed but I didn't mind. 'We are all kings and queens under the sea.'

Again came the sudden thrill, the pull like a rip-current, that I'd felt when the selkie on the shore had asked me if I wanted to hear his name under water. I recoiled so sharply that my glass slopped.

'Don't *do* that!'

'Do what?' Cal looked abashed, then closed his eyes and shook his head. 'Sorry. Like I said, this sort of thing is not all my doing. It happens.'

The fish and chips arrived. We were both hungry. We ate in salt-and-vinegar silence.

'All right,' I said at we walked back to the car, justice done to the fish-life lost to the net and the deep-fat fryer. 'You're a selkie. I'm a student. Together, we fight bureaucracy.'

Cal looked at me across the car roof.

'We don't have to fight it *today*.'

'What?'

'It's Sunday,' he said. 'We're in no rush. And it's a fine day to see the rest of the island.'

I gave him a wary look. 'Somewhere inland?'

'There's hardly any "inland" on Skye, you'll have noticed.'

'Somewhere well above the shore, at any rate.'

Cal pointed north. 'To Trotternish!'

An hour or so later we were driving through the most fractured landscape I'd ever seen. It was like another country, all jagged rocks and soaring pinnacles, with great sweeps of green grass and purple heather between the outcrops. We passed the Old Man of Storr, and stopped for a few minutes at a viewpoint car park to gaze at the pleat-like basalt columns of the aptly named Kilt Rock, until the closeness to the sea and the height of the cliff below the railing made me uneasy. We returned to the car, and Cal drove up the road over the Quiraing. At the crest of a saddle-back summit, Cal pulled over into the off-road parking area, and we got out. Sight-seers in bright cagoules dotted the wide hilltop like colourful deer.

The sun still beat relentlessly, but the air was colder up here, and the breeze stronger. It carried smells of heather and myrtle and sheep droppings. I followed Cal as he strolled to a nearby precipice. The cliff itself wasn't high, but the fall of the land in front of it was. It wasn't the height that was dizzying, but the vacancy before me, the chasms of air all around. Far below, little lochs glittered. Far across the sea, Beinn Alligin browed the clouds. Between it and me there was nothing but the same wind as plucked at my back.

'Wow,' I said, inadequately.

'Far enough from the shore for you?' Cal teased.

I turned, into the full beam of his windswept grin. It stopped my breath and skipped my heart, but something was different. Like seeing an actor in the flesh and not on the screen.

'This glamour of which you speak,' I said, 'does it depend on your closeness to the sea?'

This was a guess, but it struck.

'Yes,' said Cal. 'And more than the glamour, come to that. We cannot live for long far from the sea.'

'How far? And how long?'

'That would be telling. A good day's walk, let's say, and a

week perhaps.'

'So you're safe here,' I said. 'But the shine is off your glamour.'

It was as though his gaze turned inward. 'So it would seem.'

'Then you'll accept,' I said, 'that what I'm about to do is from me, and not from the glamour?'

'If I must,' he said.

I stepped away from the cliff and the gulf of sky, and held out my hand. He took it.

'This way,' I said.

I tugged him back along the little ridge and then, bounding and laughing, down the side of the hill and around the corner of an outcrop tens of metres down-slope. We were sheltered from the wind and from the sight of anyone nearby. I didn't care about distant walkers with binoculars.

I swung around as we stumbled to a halt, and let the momentum carry him into my arms. His lips joined to mine. We took it from there.

It's none of your business.

Oh, all right. Here are the answers to your questions.

Yes.

With most of our clothes on.

Sweet and hot.

Tongues like fishes in mouths.

I fumbled with belts and zips. He was deft. Fingers that could unknot a sea-soaked rope in the dark.

Hard, yes, and tough, like a thick, live seaweed stem.

Salt and seawater and slippery, like oysters.

I didn't count the waves that buoyed me up, and swooped me down, and after so many undulations rose to a crest that tumbled to surf and left me sprawled and spent like the hissing lace of a broken wave rushing up the sand.

Happy now?

I was.

Happy, yes, but with skin scratched and clothes with bits of heather and lichen sticking to them.

'You have sheep shit on your bum,' Cal told me.

'So have you,' I said, hand exploring. 'Fortunately it seems to be dry – oh shit, no.'

'That's just moss,' he said.

We lay on our backs and looked up at the clear blue sky. Then we tugged up our jeans and fastened our belts and stood up. Shaking, I leaned into his chest and hugged. He hugged back. We stepped apart and looked at each other.

'Well,' he said.

'Um,' I said.

'That wasn't the glamour working,' said Cal. 'I'll give you that.'

I laughed. 'What must it be like *with* the glamour working?'

Cal gave me a sudden wicked smile.

'Do you want to find out?'

'Oh my God, yes.'

We walked back to the car.

Cal drove down to the other side of the Quiraing, to a landscape flat and green and glinting with lochs, and then on over hills and moors, along main roads and then side roads and single track roads. On a crest of marram grass he stopped. We got out. There was no sound but the distant lowing of cows and the closer crash of waves. I followed him over a few more ups and downs, and suddenly we were in a small cove with a tiny sandy beach. Cal took off his T-shirt and undid his belt. I looked at him dubiously.

'You want to swim?'

'Don't you?'

'I warn you, I'll be bloody cold.'

'You won't,' he said.

We both stripped and ran into the sea.

I felt no cold at all.

The shadows were lengthening by the time we got back to Kyleakin.

'Do you want me to drop you off?'

'Not at the Crossing Lodge! In fact… would you mind showing me where you live?'

'I wouldn't mind,' said Cal. 'But you might find it a bit disillusioning.'

'As long as it isn't a cave,' I said.

He drove along the street where he'd vanished around a corner. He parked the car by the side of the road. I got out, lugging my rucksack. Right in front of us was a metre-wide gap between two adjacent garden fences. This must have been how he'd disappeared the other night. Down that narrow alley of trampled weeds we went, across some waste ground and down to the rocky shore. A small promontory lay between this part of the shore and the ferry slipway. Just above the strandline of seaweed and driftwood stood a shed with one square window. The walls were tarpaper and the roof was corrugated iron. The shed had an annexe, barely large enough to support a door, which I guessed was an outside privy. The roof had a crooked iron pipe sticking out, and a small pole at the gable onto which overhead cables ran into the hut.

Cal opened the padlock that secured the main door, and

held it open.

'Want to come in?'

'After you,' I said. I left the door open.

The inside was dark after the bright sunlight. Cal clicked a light switch and a fluorescent overhead strip flickered on. Despite its cold light the room looked cheery enough, if spartan: a single bed piled with blankets, a pot-bellied iron stove, a washbasin, a table stacked with battered paperbacks. More books were lined up on shelves, to which here and there jam jars filled with bits of sea-smoothed glass, odd pebbles and bright shells, added a decorative touch. The walls were pasted with yellowing newspapers. Sheepskins carpeted the stone floor. The whole place had a tang of wood smoke and fish.

'It's, uh, all right,' I said.

Cal looked pleased.

I waved at the light tube. 'How do you pay the electricity bill?'

'I don't,' said Cal. 'My feudal superior does.'

'You have a feudal superior? Wasn't that abolished back in the Nineties?'

Cal shrugged. 'I wouldn't know. I pay my feu at the castle every year, cash in hand, and that covers electricity and plumbing and council tax and all that.'

I didn't ask which castle. There are lots.

'Another of those arrangements?'

'Well, yes. It's of long standing.'

'Uh huh,' I said, gazing at a page of *The Scotsman* announcing Agassiz's discovery of evidence in Scotland of ancient glacier movements, and a *Daily Record* front page recording the first Moon landing. 'You've been here all this time?'

'Oh no!' said Cal. 'Just… off and on. Others have used it.'

He didn't say what others. I didn't ask.

'But it is your permanent address?'

'Yes.' He looked puzzled. 'Does that matter?'

'It does if we're going to be communicating with officialdom,' I said. 'What is the address, by the way?'

'I don't get much post,' he said. 'But "The Shed, The Shore, Kyleakin" should find me.'

'I'll make a start,' I said. 'Tonight. When will I see you again?'

'Tomorrow evening, after nine? Top of the slipway?'

'Yes,' I said. I opened my arms. 'Kiss?'

He shook his head. 'It could be dangerous here.' He didn't explain why, but he added: 'We both have… a lot to take in.'

We had indeed. With some reluctance, I hefted my rucksack, blew Cal a kiss, and ducked out into the sunlight and crunched away across the shingle beach.

Back at the Crossing Lodge, I rinsed my snorkel and flippers in the sink, sloped off to my room and showered and changed. Then I took my swimsuit and towel and grubby clothes downstairs and slung them in the washing machine. I had just clunked the door shut and was twisting the dial when Jeanie manifested behind me.

'You've been out all day?' she said, cheerily.

'Yes,' I said, standing up and forcing a smile. 'Swimming.' I gestured apologetically at the snorkel and flippers, still drying above the sink like some exotic seafood preparation.

'Aye, and gallivanting about on the hills with yon *craitur*.'

How had she known? To my annoyance, I felt myself blushing.

'Yes,' I said, more defiantly than I felt.

She looked a bit more serious, and then made a twitch of her mouth, a shrug of her cheek. 'Well, I warned you, so on your head be it, as I said.'

'I guess so,' I said. 'How did you know?'

Jeanie smiled, visibly relenting a little, and tapped the side of her nose. 'It's a small island.'

It's nothing of the sort, of course, but I left it at that. I'd already seen how the gossip network worked, now with added internet connectivity.

Some of the guests were in the front room, and the television was braying with audience laughter. I took a cup of tea and a biscuit upstairs, fired up my laptop, and did a search on naval bases. It's not easy to find the right person to talk to about selkies and submarines. After a good deal of thought I decided to use the MoD's confidential hotline email facility, and composed a polite message titled:

Welfare concerns raised by marine Metamorpha – query

In it, I briefly explained who I was, who Cal was, my encounter with the other selkie that morning, and Cal's explanation of what the selkies' problems were. Then I signed off, hit Send, and closed the laptop in the warm glow of a good deed well done.

You know what they say about good deeds.

Seven

Mr Sucky was jammed against the side of a bed and I was half way under it, probing with the brush extension at a warren's worth of dust bunnies. Somebody was shouting, but I couldn't make out what. Then the floor vibrated in sync with an agitated thunder of feet up the stairs.

'Siobhan!'

Startled, I banged my head on the flange of the bedstead, swore, dropped the metal tube and scrambled to my feet. I'd just got the vacuum switched off and my mouth shaping up to shout 'What?' when the door flew open.

'There's two men at the door for you,' said Jeanie, looking flustered.

'Men?' I said. 'Do they know me?'

'They know *about* you,' said Jeanie, grimly. 'They look official.'

'Oh!' I said. 'That's all right! I'll explain later.'

I cast off my tabard and flicked back my hair. 'Not too grubby?'

'Just *go*,' said Jeanie. 'And mind what you say.'

I shot her a raised eyebrow and hurried down the stairs. Two young men in black suits and polished shoes stood on the doorstep, fresh-faced as Mormon missionaries. Instead of tracts they clutched iPads.

'Miss Siobhan Ross?'

'That's me,' I said. 'And you?'

'We're from the Admiralty,' said one of them. 'We'd like to have a chat with you.'

'What about?'

'Your email last night.'

'Fine,' I said. 'Would you like to step inside?'

'Not really, Miss Ross,' said the other guy. 'We'd like you to come with us.'

He indicated a car parked a few metres from the gate.

I had been hoping for a quick response. This was quick, but I felt uneasy.

'I'm sorry,' I said, 'but I need to see some identification.'

They each fished out and held up cards that looked authentic, but how was I to judge?

'All right,' I said, stepping back and glancing over my shoulder. 'I'll just get my jacket and my –'

'No need,' said one of them. 'We won't be long.'

'Still –'

I turned around and stepped back into the hallway, with a wild thought of kicking the door shut and legging it out the back. Any such notions, as well as my doubts, were put to rest as a police constable ambled through from the kitchen, casually munching a sausage roll.

'Thanks Gordon!' she called over her shoulder. Then she stopped in front of me. I noticed, with a cold shock, that she had a pistol holstered on her belt. In Britain we aren't used to armed police except at airports. I remembered a minor flurry of controversy a few months earlier about its becoming routine in the Highlands and Islands.

'Go with the Admiralty men,' the PC said. 'Don't make a scene.'

I reached for my jacket. She shook her head firmly. 'As you

are.'

Baffled, I complied. Jeanie was watching from the top of the stairs, arms folded, lips compressed.

The morning was sunny with broken cloud and a stiff breeze, but these weren't what made me shiver as I walked coatless to the car. The police woman had strolled out of the gate in the opposite direction to the one the car was facing, ostentatiously making clear that she had a Taser on the back of her belt, and that she had nothing to do with what was going on (and thus, no doubt, affirming Jeanie's respectability: this wasn't an arrest, or an immigration raid, oh no).

The car was a black Nissan. One guy held the near rear door open for me. I got in and buckled up. He came around and sat beside me in the back. The other took the driver's seat. We pulled away. To my surprise, he took the road out of Kyleakin, towards Portree.

'I thought we'd be going to the mainland,' I remarked, breaking ice.

'We're not going far,' said the man beside me. I got the impression that conversation wasn't welcome. I hunched back in the seat, gazing worriedly out the windows and gloomily reflecting on how different I had felt taking the same road with Cal just the day before.

A few miles past Broadford, by the shore of a long finger of sea loch, the driver turned off on a single-track road that wended up into the hills. By the time we were a hundred metres above sea level the main road was well out of sight. Another turn-off, along a bumpy unpaved road that ran more or less horizontally along the hillside for a few hundred metres. It ended at a patch of gravel about twenty metres square that looked like the remains of a quarry, except that the three rocky sides were lichen-patched, eroded cliffs. As the car halted, it struck me that the cubical hollow could indeed be a quarry: one so ancient you couldn't tell it from natural rock.

A concrete bunker abutted the inner cliff. It had no windows and one door. The man beside me jumped out, nipped around the rear of the car and had the door open for me before I'd got the seatbelt properly off.

Outside, the wind plucked at my shirt and flicked at my hair.

'This way,' said the driver, as if there was any other.

One on either side of me, they walked me to the bunker. The door swung outward silently as we approached. A man in a stiff naval uniform ushered us inside. The door was of metal, about ten centimetres thick, and with a flange all around and along the side half a dozen retracted bolts gleaming with oil. It clunked shut behind us like a bank safe.

Inside the bunker was a meeting room of sorts, with plastic chairs around the walls and a long table down the middle with a shaded strip-light hanging over it. There was a water cooler, a coffee machine, and a recycling bin. Whiteboards on every wall, with well-used coloured pens filling the gutter shelves beneath. At the far end was a door.

'Welcome to HMS *Cuillin*, Miss Ross,' said the naval officer. 'Pull up a seat.'

I sat down. The naval officer stood. The Admiralty men departed through the inner door. I glimpsed a concrete-walled, strip-lit corridor beyond. After a minute the door opened again. The naval officer snapped to attention as a much more senior officer came in. His face was wrinkled and tanned. His cap carried a cluster of braid and his jacket a palette of medal ribbons. Not quite knowing what was appropriate, I stood up.

He leaned over the table and shook my hand, then smiled wryly.

'Please sit down, Miss Ross.' His accent was English, with a Scottish undertow.

'Thank you, uh, sir.'

He chuckled. 'Please call me John.' He said it as it were the first name that had popped into his head.

'Siobhan,' I said, sitting.

He took off his cap, revealing close-cropped white hair, and took a seat opposite me. After a nod from him, his junior sat at a far corner, pen poised over a Moleskine.

'Is this a secret base?' I said, trying to sound insouciant.

The senior officer smiled, the junior officer suppressed a snort.

'Shore base HMS *Cuillin*,' John told me solemnly, 'is not secret.' He shrugged his epaulettes. 'The Russians know it, Wikileaks knows it, even CND knows it. It doesn't appear on any public list or maps, however.'

'I see,' I said, none the wiser.

'Now, to business.' John took a folded sheet of paper from a breast pocket, and spread it open on the table. He spun it around with his finger and slid it across. 'This is the email you sent?'

I peered at the print-out.

'That's what I wrote,' I said. 'I can't vouch for the headers.'

John laughed. 'You don't have to! Very well. Now, Siobhan, I want to make quite clear that you are not in trouble. Not with us, at any rate. But... If you don't answer fully and truthfully, you will be.'

'I've nothing to hide,' I said.

'Good.' He put his elbows on the table and his clasped knuckles to his lips, and studied me for a moment. Then he opened his hands.

'So tell me,' he said, 'if you have had sexual relations with either of the two beings you encountered.'

I sat up straight in the chair, and took a deep breath. 'I've had sexual relations with Cal.'

'And the other one?'

'No!'

'How did the one you call Cal approach you?'

'It was more like I approached him,' I said. 'He even warned me off.'

John gave the junior officer a glance that said told-you-so.

'They're getting quite canny in that respect,' he said.

'What do you mean by that?' I asked.

He ignored the question, and asked another.

'Under what circumstances,' he asked, 'did your sexual relations take place? Let me spare your blushes – I don't want a, ah, blow by blow account. Just time and place.'

I told him, unblushingly. By the end he looked a little warm himself.

'This all took place *yesterday*?'

'Yes.'

'How long have you known this Cal?'

I told him that, too. He leaned back, and sighed.

'Well, I'm not your father,' he said. 'And you're an adult, otherwise unattached. If this Cal were a human being, of any sex, colour or creed or… well, and so on and so forth, I'd have nothing to reproach you with. Clear?'

'Yes,' I said. 'I'm sensing a "but" coming.'

'*However*,' he said, 'you must be well aware that he is not human. And that makes all the difference.'

'So everyone keeps telling me.'

'Oh yes,' he said. 'Starting with your esteemed employer Mrs McIntyre, no doubt, and continuing through any kirk elders you may have encountered in passing?'

'Something like that,' I said.

'Indeed,' said John, heavily. 'People you can dismiss as superstitious old –'

'No, no, I don't –'

'While, I'm sure, your young colleagues at the Crossing Lodge think it's all very romantic.'

'To the extent that they know about it,' I said. 'But as I was saying, I don't think Jeanie – Mrs McIntyre – is what you said, at all. She's just, well –'

I flailed, trying to think of a way to put it politely.

'Exactly,' said John. 'And I'm at a like disadvantage, I expect.'

I shook my head firmly. 'No, sir, nothing like that. You're a naval officer, you must know what you're talking about.'

'I sometimes wish that followed,' he said, as if to the table, or himself. Then he looked up sharply. 'But in this case, Siobhan, I do know what I'm talking about. My rank wouldn't mean much to you if you can't read it off my pips, but I have certain academic qualifications and three decades of field experience. And going by your email and what we've been able to find out about you since someone read it this morning, you're someone who takes both science and national security – which is to say, the safety and wellbeing of your country – seriously.'

'Well, yes, of course,' I said. I did a little double take. '"Field experience"? You've *worked* with selkies?'

John scratched an eyebrow. 'No comment. I can neither confirm nor deny, et cetera. Okay?'

'Okay,' I said. 'I'm listening.'

'Coffee,' said John, with a wave at the junior officer. That sorted, he proceeded.

'Well, Siobhan, you've evidently read up on selkies and the other metamorpha, you know the current state of public and common knowledge about them, so you must know the limits of that. Correct?'

'Yes, well,' I said, a little uncomfortably, 'it's kind of obvious that there's been hardly any open research in the past century, but they're so interesting and… perplexing that there must be *some* scientific research, so if we don't know about it, it must be secret. I've always assumed it was military.'

'You assumed right,' he said. 'And I'm not about to tell you anything covered by the Official Secrets Act. It's been discovered and confirmed by defence-related research, true enough, but I think you'll find it's consistent with what you can work out for yourself from what you already know, including from what your friend Cal and the other selkie have told you.'

'Uh-huh.'

'The selkies – sticking to them for the moment – are not native to this planet, and perhaps not to this universe. Agreed?'

'Well, they say that too,' I said.

John nodded. 'And they've been here a long time. We don't know how many millions of years, but we do know this: they were here *before us*. Before humanity. Yes?'

'Well,' I said brightly, 'the fossil record is –'

John raised a hand. 'Please. Their fossil record is quite a bit richer than you'll find in textbooks, or even journals. I've seen rocks with my own eyes that… I sometimes wish I hadn't. Take it from me, Siobhan, these things were around before the apes, let alone us. They *emulated* native life, as they still do. Fish. Seals. Dolphins. With me so far?'

'Yes,' I said.

'Okay. Now, you wouldn't say a selkie is *actually* a school of fish, or a seal, or a porpoise, even if its emulation of them is good enough to fool fish and marine mammals themselves. The same applies to a selkie emulating a human being. It's like – you know about the Turing Test?'

'Of course I know about it,' I said.

'Fine, fine. Well then – think of the selkie as an alien, or as an artificial intelligence. Perhaps even both: an extraterrestrial artificial intelligence. Which is one hypothesis, as it happens. But whatever the truth of that, we can be sure of this. The human appearance is a *front-end*, an avatar, of something that is quite inhuman in its real working.'

'But Cal explained this to me,' I said. 'It's not like that.'

'Oh?'

'He said that people think the selkie is the real self, and the human an avatar, or a mask, but it isn't like that at all. He says he feels like a human being all the way through, but the selkie is like… something larger he's part of and as Cal doesn't fully understand or control.'

'Yes, exactly, Siobhan! That's what I'm saying. When Cal says his appearance is not an avatar, he means it's not like some character you control in a computer game. He doesn't feel himself to be some kind of mind behind the scenes, pulling the strings of the handsome, charming lad you know as Cal. I can well believe he's telling the truth as he understands it. He, in his inmost self as Cal, is not the puppet master. He's the puppet.'

My palms were wet and my stomach cold. And then heat spread from my cheeks to my shoulders. Anger drove me to reach for any knowledge that could help. I found it, strangely, in a memory of First Year English.

'Isn't that true of all of us?' I said, my voice shaking only a little. 'Our brains and bodies and language work us in ways that have very little to do with what we think is our *inmost self.*' I shrugged. 'If Cal is a puppet of something not human, so am I and so are you.'

'Yes,' said John, mildly. 'But at least ours are human brains and bodies and languages, which evolved on this Earth. You must admit that makes a difference.'

'Yes,' I conceded. 'But –'

'So spare me your undergraduate post-structuralism, Miss Ross. I'm not some salty old skipper with nothing but navigation grades on his ticket.'

'I never –'

'Okay, I take that back. But listen, please. Whatever you feel about Cal, and whatever Cal feels about himself and you, something else – the deep selkie self – is manipulating him, and through him is manipulating *you.*'

I took a deep breath. 'If he is, or it is, that's none of your business, is it?'

'It wasn't,' John said grimly, 'until you sent that email. That made it our business all right. Because that email was *them*, the selkies, or some of them, trying to manipulate *us*, the Royal Navy no less!'

He sounded so indignant that I was taken aback.

'But all I've done,' I said hotly, 'is raise a concern that was put to me by a selkie who seems to represent some body of opinion among selkies that the Navy doesn't usually hear. This was confirmed and clarified by a selkie I know personally. There was no manipulation in that. There's nothing sinister about it. The selkies are recognised under the Treaty of St Kilda. I'm a British subject and a UK citizen and I have the right to respectfully petition the lawful authorities, have I not?'

'As I said, Miss Ross, you are not in trouble. Not with us, and not for what you did. But I'm sorry to say you're in serious danger of *getting* into trouble. It's not so much the emotional thing – and there, I'm afraid, the old tales are all too true, this can only end in heartbreak, but as you say that's your risk to take – but the security aspect. Which is why we're here.'

'Is there a security aspect?' I looked from one officer to the other, alarmed. The junior officer kept his head down, scribbling assiduous shorthand. 'What?'

'Because the' – John took a deep breath – 'dissident selkies, if we can call them that, are interfering with *our bloody submarines*!' He banged a hand on the table, then seemed to repent of his wrath. 'Excuse my language, Miss Ross, but this is a serious matter. That creature you spoke to at the beach gave a heavy hint – and a credible one, I'm free to tell you – that they had *grounded* one of our subs just the other week. That grounding off Kyleakin before the eyes of the world was deeply embarrassing, and is the subject of a full inquiry. Disciplinary, operational, political, the lot. The information you've given us could save more than one career. If it can be verified – I'll come back to that – it means that no incompetence by those concerned with navigating and/or driving the boat was to blame. But it also means that these selkies have demonstrated a capacity and will to sabotage our last line of defence. You mentioned the Treaty of St Kilda, Miss Ross. I suggest you read it. Any interference in naval operations is strictly ruled out.'

'But if they did anything,' I said, 'they only raised a sandbar! It's hardly a surprise they can do that, and –'

'It *is* a surprise,' said the junior officer, suddenly chipping in. 'Think about it. We're talking hundreds of cubic metres of sand and gravel. The selkies have unusual powers, but they can't do that sort of thing by magic. And doing it in –'

His superior shot him a warning glance. He nodded and continued. 'In the time frame implied by, ah, our records, would require the co-operation of scores of selkies at least. That's unprecedented, in our experience. And their foreknowledge of where the boat would go raises other disturbing questions. No, this isn't a trivial matter at all.'

'I quite see that,' I said. 'But from their point of view, surely, it's more like civil disobedience – well, okay, direct action, like the Faslane protests – than sabotage. They have a grievance, and they claim that your, I mean our, submarines are going into areas of sea that the Treaty excludes them from.' I made wiping movements with my hands. 'No, I don't know where these are, and I don't want to, as I told the selkie. The point is, they say that they have no way of being heard, because the only ones the Navy hears from are the ones who work *with* the Navy, so they had to do something to draw attention to their grievance.'

'Who made you their lawyer?' John growled.

'I'm *not* their lawyer,' I said. 'I'm just relaying to you what they – well, two of them – told me.'

'Well seen you're not their lawyer,' said the younger officer.

'If you were, you'd have read the Treaty. It specifically says that submarines can go where they want.'

'No doubt,' I said, digging my heels in. 'But in those days submarines were just, what, U-boats? New and unfamiliar and running on diesel. And according to Cal, there are marine exclusion zones that have been demarcated since, which the subs and lots of other undersea activity are encroaching on.'

'Again, have you read the documents establishing these exclusion zones?'

'Well, no, but Cal says they're secret anyway.'

'Secret they may be,' said John. 'But I can tell you this. Do you imagine that HMG, the MoD, the Admiralty, or the Royal Navy, would countenance for a moment any restrictions on where our submarines go? The whole point of a submarine is that it can go undetected until the last moment. That was true in the early days of U-boats, it's true of our hunter-killer subs today, and it's a thousand times truer in the case of our nuclear deterrent.'

'I don't see how a few marine exclusion zones can affect that,' I said.

'For heaven's sake!' John said. 'Do I have to draw you a map? Very well, then.'

He jumped up and stalked out, to return an awkward minute later with a chart, which he spread out on the table. The chart showed the seas around the west coast of Scotland. John stabbed at it with his finger. 'Islands. Sea lochs. Firths. Channels and sounds. Major shipping routes. Faslane and the other bases. Take a good look at channel depths, and you'll see how it's all a watery maze of passages to the Irish Sea and the Atlantic. Now, start blanking off great areas of that.' He moved his fingertip around, vaguely sketching in long blocks here and there. 'You see? If an opponent knows where our boats *aren't*, they have a much better chance of figuring out where they *are*.'

'But if the restricted areas are secret –'

'They'd be a lot harder to keep secret than the course of a submarine voyage,' John pointed out. 'Assuming for the sake of argument that they exist.'

I pondered the map. 'But even so, the possible routes are still miles wide. You'd need an enormous explosion to… oh.'

'"Oh", indeed,' said John grimly. 'If, God forbid, we were ever in a situation where taking out a Trident sub would be on an opponent's list of things to do today, using one nuke to prevent the launch of… a whole lot more might look like a bargain.' He brushed his hands with a couple of brisk claps. 'So let's stop messing about, shall we? This dissident selkie business is serious. We can't meet their demands, and the very fact that they've made them, and their action in grounding the sub, shows that they're culpably casual about our national security at the very least, and actively disloyal at worst.'

I must have looked shocked. 'But surely – I mean, how can you expect selkies to know about nuclear deterrence?'

John glared. 'Because the selkies we work with know. Those who don't work with us know at second hand. Before you make any further objections, let me add that the last thing you can call selkies is *naïve*. The ones who work with us' – he closed his eyes firmly for a moment, shook his head, and sighed – 'they're not like trained dolphins, or police dogs. They have the same understanding of what they're doing as human personnel of equivalent rank. Maybe more – as you'll have noticed with your new boyfriend, selkies have a thirst for knowledge and a shrewd grasp of affairs. The same must go for the dissidents. They're not some woolly-hat peace campers, I'll tell you that for nothing.'

The coffee had gone cold, and had never tasted very good anyway.

'What are they, then?' I demanded. 'Russian special ops?'

'There is that possibility,' said John, not sounding as if he believed it. 'The bottom line is that they're hostile. Whether they have now or might consider in future some alignment with other hostiles is neither here nor there. They are a power, of unknown intent, in our oceans and coastal seas. And you, Miss Ross, are in grave danger of becoming their pawn.'

'That's my problem,' I said, 'as you keep admitting! And if your problem is that the selkies who disagree with the Navy might be hostile, why don't you get your loyal selkies on their case?'

The junior officer snorted. John gave him an odd glance, as if seeking permission, then said: 'Really, Miss Ross! As I said, our selkies aren't like trained animals, and they aren't like native allies either. Every one of them is an ancient, alien power, with a will of its own that sometimes coincides with ours, and sometimes doesn't. The coincidence of interests between some of them and us is not something to put under strain. Selkies are vulnerable to some of our measures, as you know, but not to each other's. You can't fight selkies with selkies, any more than you can fight water with water. And they have no *loyalty* to us. But you, I hope, do.'

'And supposing my greater loyalty's to the selkies whose case I've raised?'

'If we thought that,' John said, in a tone of idle speculation, 'you'd leave this room through that door.' He jerked his thumb at the door into the rock. 'And if you give us good reason to think otherwise, you leave through the door you came in, free as a bird. Your choice.'

He stared at me. I stared down at the table. I had never been sold on the nuclear deterrent, but I had no interest in helping some hostile power, human or otherwise. How I felt about the country was complicated, and I knew well enough that the country isn't the same as the state. But now the question was being put point blank, in very much more fraught circumstances than an argument in a Student Union bar. I felt isolated, dismayed, and confused. But I wasn't crushed. I looked up, and tried not to look at the door into the rock.

'So,' I said, 'what do you want me to do?'

'It's very simple,' said John. 'We want you to keep us in the picture. I'll show you how.'

Eight

The two Admiralty men drove me back to the Crossing Lodge. I made no attempt at conversation. We stopped a few gates away from the house, and one of the operatives got out and opened the back door.

'Thank you,' I said.

'You're welcome.'

I walked to the gate of the Lodge. The car stayed where it was. As I went through the door I heard the engine start up. Out of the corner of my eye, I saw the car go past as I closed the door behind me.

The smell of Brasso and Pledge, recently applied (by me). The ticking clock. A bouquet of furled umbrellas, now dry. A framed antique map of Kyleakin. For a moment I stood in the hallway, remembering how homely it had seemed the day I arrived. If I thought a minute more I would cry. I walked briskly into the kitchen. Jeanie and Gordon were at the table with coffee and sandwiches.

'What was all that about?' Gordon asked.

Jeanie frowned at him briefly, and then raised her eyebrows to me. 'Are you all right, Siobhan?'

'I'm fine,' I said, making for the kettle. 'I sent the Navy a query about selkies and submarines, and they got all sniffy about it.' I shrugged. 'Just a misunderstanding, you know how twitchy officials can be these days. Security and all that. Anyway, it's all cleared up now.'

The kettle boiled, the switch clicked off. I poured hot water onto instant and added a drop of cold. My hand wasn't shaking a bit.

'Are you sure?' Jeanie asked.

'Don't worry,' I said. 'You won't have Men in Black turning up at the door again.'

I sat down at the table.

'Does that mean you won't be seeing Cal again?' Gordon asked. Another frown from Jeanie.

'Oh no!' I said brightly. 'They're quite happy with me seeing Cal. Like I said, just a misunderstanding. Something got blown out of proportion.'

Jeanie was looking at me intently. 'What did you ask about submarines?'

I gave her the most sincere smile I could muster. 'Well, that's just the trouble, you see. I kind of… asked an awkward question and it turned out I'd stumbled on some big hush-hush stuff, and I've had to swear blind I won't talk about it to anyone ever again. And I think that has to include you, Jeanie, sorry.'

She didn't look convinced, or pleased. 'Well, I'm hardly a security risk!'

'Sorry,' I said. 'But they were very insistent.'

'I bet it had to do with yon sub that grounded last week,' said Gordon.

'My lips are zipped,' I told him, followed by the accompanying gesture.

Jeanie took a deep breath through her nose, and exhaled a sigh.

'Ah,' she said. 'Well, let's leave it there. I'm glad you're all right and everything's fine. Now, when you finish your coffee, dear, there's a stack of sheets to iron.'

'After this morning,' I said, quite truthfully for a change, 'I'll be glad to get back to them.'

In the windowless laundry room behind the kitchen, I faced a heap of still-warm sheets in front of the tumble dryer and summoned my resolution. Maybe some tears fell on the odd sheet, but at least I didn't drip snot. Ironing sheets is tedious and awkward, especially in such a confined space, but the good thing was I could do it while thinking about something else.

John and his nameless sidekick had caught me and entangled me. The worst part was that I had no one to talk to. I didn't dare phone or text my friends. I thought for a moment of messaging apps with end-to-end encryption, but I didn't know if my phone – which I hadn't been allowed to take with me that morning – had itself somehow been compromised. Face-to-face, heart-to-heart didn't look promising either. Jeanie could be counted on to disapprove. Mairi might well feel quite the opposite but with the best will in the world I couldn't see her as a fount of wise advice. And Kieran – setting aside the emotional aftermath and his social cluelessness – could hardly be relied on to be objective.

The ironing done, I found Gordon at the kitchen table, frowning over the evening menu and a stack of cookery books opened at smudged pages.

'I always have to work out the quantities every time,' he said, looking up with a half apologetic smile. Then he stood up, looking serious. 'What's the matter?'

'Oh, it's – it's –' All the tears I'd been holding back welled up and burst out.

Suddenly I was sobbing into his shoulder and he had his arms around me.

'Come on outside,' he said, stepping back.

I glanced over my shoulder.

'Have we got some privacy?'

He grinned. 'Jeanie's at the shops.'

I followed him out the back door into the sun-trap of the garden. There was a bench dry enough to sit on against the house wall. Gordon sat down and lit up; I sat down and wished for a reckless moment that I smoked.

'So,' Gordon said, 'what's the story?'

He got through two cigarettes as I told him.

'Hm,' he mused when I'd shuddered to a halt, 'that's tricky.'

I sniffed hard. Bees clambered around the wisteria on the garden wall.

'Well,' Gordon said at last, 'you really have got yourself in a fankle. The British state is the original iron fist in the velvet glove. They're not going to let you go. And on the other side…' He looked up at me, shook his head, and sighed. 'Selkies, huh. Of all the things. How could you let yourself get caught in *their* nets?'

'But you knew I meant to go out with Cal! Only Jeanie objected, you and Mairi were all like ooh ah lucky you if you can get him interested.'

'It isn't *that*,' said Gordon, witheringly. 'All your oceanic orgasmic stuff might be worth heartbreak at the end, that's up to you. I'd be tempted myself, if any was on offer. It's acting as a… a *conduit* for them, for their political wiles. As soon as you agreed to sort of represent them, as soon as you hit Send on that email… Oh, Siobhan, couldn't you see where that might lead?'

'No,' I said. 'The old stories have nothing to say about

that.'

He looked at me as if I was an idiot, or maybe just in gobsmacked surprise, then smiled sadly. 'You're a Sassenach, that's the trouble. You haven't heard *enough* old stories. They're not all about doomed lovers, you know. There are tales about chiefs who get offered alliances with selkies, to cross a sea or attack a fleet or whatever, and how it never works out well for them.'

'It's the Navy should be worried about that side of it,' I said bitterly.

'And so they are, by the sounds of it,' said Gordon.

'That's not a lot of help to me,' I said.

Gordon jumped to his feet. 'It is and all,' he said. He frowned at me for a moment. 'You haven't *sworn* anything, have you?'

I thought back to what I'd agreed with John and the other guy. 'No,' I said. 'I haven't even signed the Official Secrets Act.'

He smacked a fist on a palm. 'Awesome!' he said. 'So just tell all to Cal.'

'What?'

'Why not? He'll understand.'

I was none too sure about that.

At quarter to nine that evening I slipped out of the house in the charity-shop floaty flowery skirt and the sound walking shoes and a warm jacket, under a lemon sky. I was out for a date and a scramble. The breeze that had cooled the hot day persisted, which cheered me further because it meant there'd be no midges.

The latest surge of cars tailed a coach up the road from the slipway. Outside the Castle Rock the old man – Uilleam, Cal had called him – drew hard on a roll-up, and looked right through me as I hurried past.

Cal was sitting on a bollard, legs stretched out in front of him. He got to his feet when he saw me, and strode to meet me. We hugged.

'Well, hello,' he said, stepping back with a grin.

'Hello,' I said.

'Where do you want to go?'

'Let's take a walk along the shore,' I said.

He gave me a curious look. 'The tide's out, and the seaweed's stinking.'

'I don't mind.'

He shrugged. 'Fine.'

Hand in hand, we walked along the shingle at the top of the beach, above the strandline. A few days around the neap tides had left seaweed in heaps to cake in the sun and soak in the rain, and they stank all right. Clouds of small insects hovered above them. Cal kicked at driftwood and once or twice stooped to pick up and pocket a nub of sea-glass, blue or green or grey-white.

'Adding to your collection?'

'I like to look at them,' he said. 'Sand gets made into glass, which gets broken and thrown away, and sometimes the shards are ground into pebbles by the waves, and some day these glass pebbles will be embedded in sand that becomes rock, and some of that rock will be lifted and eroded to become cliffs, and the broken rock will become pebbles again, with the glass pebbles inside. And some of that rock will be worn away by rivers, and become sand again and pile up on beaches. And maybe that sand will be made into glass. And maybe a selkie will pick up one of those pebbles, and remember this moment, and you asking.'

I clutched his hand, hard. 'You expect to live that long?

Millions of years?'

He laughed. 'Not me personally, not Cal. But the selkie self could, and it might keep some of my memories it likes, that it holds onto like yon smooth bits of coloured glass.'

'Jeez. That's… cold.'

'It's better than most people can hope for.'

I wasn't sure if he meant me or him. We walked on for a bit, past his shack without a glance.

'So,' he said, 'what d'you want to talk about, that's so secret?'

I didn't need to ask how he knew. I'd never have taken him on this long and awkward traipse otherwise. The thought of a bright noisy bar where we could talk nonsense like normal people was suddenly overwhelming. But needs must.

I scoped out a couple of adjacent boulders and plodded towards them, then sat down on one and beckoned Cal to sit facing me. Which he did, knees to knees. The lichen was prickly through the thin fabric of my skirt, the wind off the sea cold on my face. Across the water, the lights of Kyle of Lochalsh were winking on.

'It's about this morning,' I said. I told him what had happened, up until my capitulation.

'And then what did they ask you to do?' he said.

I took a deep breath, and gazed up at the yellow sky. 'They told me to continue seeing you, and to find out as much as I could about what the officer called "dissident selkies". And to report back to him regularly – they gave me a number for a secure line.'

'And were you supposed to tell me this?'

'Of course not. I was very specifically told not to. They want me to *spy* on you.'

'And you agreed?'

'I had no choice.'

'I've been given to understand,' said Cal, in the tone of one making a casual observation, 'that human beings have free will. So you did have a choice.'

'Not much of a one.' I was in no mood for philosophy.

'Fair enough. Anyway, you made the right choice. And I think they fully expected you to tell me all about it.'

'What?' The dilemma I'd posed to Gordon, and the bold solution he'd suggested, seemed suddenly undercut. 'They expected me to tell you? They assumed I was lying to them?'

'Oh, Siobhan,' said Cal. 'You're too scrupulous. Whatever about free will, anything you say under coercion can't be held against you. And of course they expected it. They wanted you to tell me.'

'Why?'

'Lines of communication. They now have a deniable two-way channel to me and my kind, with you as a cut-out. That's worth more than any spy.'

This sounded plausible, yet all too convenient.

'Maybe,' I said. 'But that's not the real problem.'

Cal blinked and leaned back. 'It isn't?'

'No,' I said, 'the real problem is that I kind of think the Navy guy has a point.'

'Why?'

'From all you've told me yourself…'

Cal smiled. 'Ah, I see. Well, I do understand that. We are alien, we are powerful, and some of us have a contention with the Royal Navy. That doesn't make us hostile. If we were hostile…'

Cal stood up and stepped away, his worn-out trainers making almost no sound on the shingle. It was his voice that grated.

'If we were *hostile*,' he said, 'do you think any ship would ever sail? Do you think a coracle would ever have crossed the sea? Do you think any of their submarines would be safe? They would not just have their cursed bombs to worry about, I can tell you that!'

Cal loomed black against the ruddy glimmer of the evening sea.

'Well, yes,' I said. 'It's the possibility of your *becoming* hostile that the Navy is worried about. They have an idea of how much damage you could do if you were. They saw that grounding last week as a warning.'

Cal wasn't finished. 'You said they told you they're worried that those of us who don't work with the Navy might work with *other* navies, other powers...' He laughed. 'That isn't even insulting. Do they think it's some *accident* that their Crown has a treaty with us? And that no other power has?' He turned about, with a sweep of his arm. 'These are our seas. We've lived and swum around these islands since before the mainland *was* an island. We basked on the shores of Doggerland, and swam its forests as they sank. Wherever we came from, however long ago, this land and its waters are our home. Were we to leave it, could we find a better deal elsewhere? From the Russians? The Japanese? The Americans? We know little and care less for your politics and nations. There's only one nation we've ever fought for, the one that grew on the land our seas surround. If we go to other shores we'll not soon make a treaty with those inland. And if we go, what other allies of our like does this island have?' He shrugged, and looked around as if searching. 'The kelpies? The forest wraiths? Sadly few, ever fewer, and never strong to start with. The sky-sprites? Good luck with them! Flighty they seem, and flighty they are.' He paused, frowning. 'They could confuse enemy radar, I'll give you that, but their attention span is short. You might as well set the will-o'-the-wisp in marching order. No, we would not be disloyal. We would not serve another sovereign power, but yours would feel our loss.'

The name that came to my mind as he spoke was Albion. I could almost see it, a sleeping giant in the dusk-red skyline of the Torridon hills. Some wordless intelligence in the ancient rocks, now to be left without a host of friends.

Albion unguarded. The thought scared me more than John's talk of deterrence.

'No!' I cried. 'You can't, you can't –'

I stood up, and stepped towards Cal. As my boots crunched on the shingle a squeal like a feedback howl came from my shoulder bag. I stopped, perplexed and startled, and rummaged for the source. The strange noise was coming from my phone, which felt warm in my hand. I thumbed the screen and at first saw nothing amiss. Then I noticed that the battery was half drained. The symbol had been bright green when I'd taken the phone off the charger just before I went out.

'What's the matter?' Cal asked.

'Something's gone wrong with my phone,' I said, checking that I didn't have any apps running. The noise continued. 'Is this the kind of thing that happens around you and phones?'

'Well, kind of,' said Cal. 'But only when I try to use one. You weren't *recording* me, were you?'

'Of course not!' I said, stung by his suddenly suspicious tone. 'I wouldn't do that without telling you.'

'Your phone might do that,' Cal said, 'without telling *you*.'

I stared at him. 'I did think something like that was possible,' I said. 'That's why I haven't phoned anyone about all this.' The sound was beginning to annoy me. I switched the phone off, and stuck it back in my bag.

'Well, that's that taken care of,' I said.

Cal said nothing.

'What do you want to do now?' I asked.

Cal shrugged. 'We both know where we stand,' he said. 'We have to sort this out. We're not going to do that out here, right now. And I need to… consult.' He closed his eyes and rubbed his forehead. 'What do you want to do?'

'Go back and get a drink,' I said firmly. 'Anywhere but the

Old Castle.'

'Fine!' he said. 'The Haakon's Arms it is.' He took my hand, and squeezed it. 'We'll be all right.'

At that moment I believed we would.

'This is *our* table,' I said, swinging my legs around the end of the bench and sitting down. 'The one you once threatened to score with your claws. Isn't that romantic?'

Cal gave me a blank look. 'What would you like to drink?'

'Um… a Malibu with cranberry juice.'

He mimed a shudder and went off, to glance back with a grin at my appreciative laugh.

The pub was about half-full, mostly visitors as far as I could tell. The music was Gaelic and just loud enough to be heard above the din. I shrugged off my warm jacket and began to relax. What had seemed an impossible dilemma that afternoon had become simply a problem, to be worked out.

All I had to do was convince an unknown number of shape-shifting entities whose lives spanned geological time that they should put up with a bit of noise pollution for the sake of the island they claimed long attachment to, and to convince a hard-bitten old Naval officer and some shadowy intelligence agency I'd never heard so much as a rumour of that these shifty beings were not disloyal in objecting to nuclear submarines invading their space. There was room here for negotiation, surely. That I was in a relationship with one of these entities and probably under his glamour – willingly or not, on both sides – wouldn't hopelessly compromise me as a go-between. It was something John et al would have to take into consideration, no more and no less, a factor like any other.

Aye, dream on, Siobhan!

And while I'd been heartfelt in my reminiscence about the pub, I recalled too the dirty looks Cal had got that night. As I was scanning for any of the lads who'd stared at him, the door burst open. It was Kieran. He strode into the room and looked anxiously around. He saw me at once, looked relieved, and walked purposefully towards my corner. I gave him my best effort at resting bitch face. He ignored this and kept glancing back at the door until he stopped and leaned a hand on the table.

'What,' I said, 'the actual fuck is it this time?'

His brow was shining with sweat and he was breathing harder than usual.

'The cops are looking for you,' he said.

'Ha ha,' I said.

'They think your selkie boyfriend has kidnapped you, or something.'

'What?' Then I remembered turning off the phone. 'Oh, shit –'

I was scrabbling through my bag and Kieran was saying something about having legged it here from the Old Castle where the cops were asking around and some *bodach* talking to them and out of the corner of my eye I could see with relief Cal heading my way with a pint and a tall glass and a determined look when the swing doors burst open and two bulky figures in chequered caps and yellow hi-vis marched in and a loud voice said 'Freeze!'

I froze. So did Cal, his hands holding the two glasses conspicuously out in front of him. Kieran stood poised, half-turned from the table, knees slightly bent. The pub fell silent except for the music, incongruously reeling on.

'Put the glasses down,' said one cop. 'Then raise your hands.'

Cal swivelled about like a robot and laid the pint and the glass of pink stuff on a nearby table, then straightened, hands still held out in front of them.

'Higher,' said the cop, taking a step forward.

As Cal raised his hands it seemed that gloves had grown on them, or the skin had darkened and thickened. His nails extended and became more rounded and prominent. His face, too, was changing by the second. There was the sound of a score of people all breathing in at once. Several people raised their phones to record the scene.

The cops both reached behind their backs. A moment later, they each had a Taser levelled.

'Stop *doing* that!' said one of the cops.

Cal cast me a sidelong glance, frantic, apologetic. He barely turned his head, but his left eye seemed to be looking at me. Then he looked straight ahead.

'I can't,' he said. His voice and articulation sounded like nothing I had heard from him, or anyone. There was something the matter with his mouth.

The two cops glanced at each other. One of them spoke into his shoulder phone, then nodded. The other brought her right hand up to steady her right wrist.

'Final warning,' she said.

Cal raised his clawed hands higher, but it looked more a threat than surrender.

I wish I could say that I sprang forward between Cal and the Tasers just before they fired, and took their full shocks and fell thrashing on the floor, cracking my head on the edge of a table on the way down.

I can't.

It was Kieran who did that.

Cal, at the same moment, changed, or completed his change into something else. Where Cal had been was a thing of shells and scales, and spikes that stuck through rags and tatters of clothing, in a shape only human in some ancestral sense, a perplexity from the Burgess Shale. Head down, it charged through the sudden swift parting in the crowd, and out through the swing doors.

Everyone's gasps came out in screams.

I was kneeling on the floor beside Kieran, blood puddled around his head, and screaming at the two cops holding the other ends of the Taser wires and talking into their shoulder mikes.

'Get an ambulance! Get an ambulance!'

After a moment the male cop squatted down and shoved me aside and started giving Kieran CPR.

'Don't move his head!' said the other cop.

Kieran coughed and moved his head and opened his eyes.

'Don't move,' said the male cop. Kieran's eyes closed again.

It seemed a long time later that two guys rushed in with a hard stretcher and carried Kieran out, but it was two minutes. You can find the recordings online.

Nine

'This situation,' said Jeanie, 'has got *completely out of hand*.'

I almost laughed. It came out as something between a croak and a sob.

'You could say that.' I sniffed hard, and wiped my nose on the back of my wrist. Jeanie handed me a tissue, and I dabbed.

I was huddled on a chair in the kitchen of the Crossing Lodge, wrapped in a bedspread and sipping sugar-spiked black tea that smelled of whisky. The time was about half past ten. It can't have been more than twenty minutes after the incident. Kieran was being blue-lighted to Broadford. Cal, from what I'd heard as the police woman had bundled me up the road, had hurtled straight to the artificial inlet behind the Haakon's Arms and dived in and swum out to sea in a form like a dolphin, aquatic and streamlined and fast. Some pursuit was being attempted in a police speedboat. I had no worries about that chase being anything but futile.

My phone, now back on, was dinging constantly. I didn't dare look. I was already a hashtag.

'Tell me what happened today,' Jeanie said. 'And yesterday, while you're at it.'

I had nothing better to do, so I told her. This took me about fifteen minutes.

She poured me another cup of tea, stirred in two spoonfuls of sugar and added a hefty slug of whisky (supermarket own-brand; she was too canny to waste the good stuff on a toddy). She made the same for herself, without the sugar or the tea. She took a sip and straightened up.

'I have a wee confession to make to you,' she said. She paused. 'I don't suppose it can do any harm now. When you were being hurried out of here this morning, the police woman had your phone in her pocket already. I had told her where to find it. While you were out, she came back and returned it, and I put it back where it was.'

'So that's how they did it,' I said.

'She must have taken it to someone who put a bug in it or cloned it or whatever it is they do, and all the time afterwards your phone was transmitting everything you said. When the power got turned off, they must have suspected the worst, one way or another, and alerted the police in Kyle to come over and search for you and take Cal into custody.'

'What a mess,' I said. 'And it's all my fault.'

'There's only one thing for it,' Jeanie said. 'We'll have to sing the selkies in from the sea again, for a new meeting of them with the Navy.'

'"We"?' I stared at her. 'Do you – do you have St Kildan ancestry or what? Or are you –?'

Jeanie set her tea-cup of whisky down on the table, and sighed heavily.

'No, my dear, I am not a witch. I'm not even a wise woman. And ancestry has nothing to do with it. It's just experience and tradition.'

'Oh!' I said, suddenly hopeful. 'And you have that!'

Jeanie laughed. 'You're imagining the wee-wifies-wi'-wi-fi network of the island, and me summoning secret singers of the selkies from forgotten crofts and remote glens?'

I blushed. 'I suppose, yes.'

She shook her head. 'There's nothing like that. Well, there are some folk with the sight and so on, but I don't know more of them than you do. But they're not needed anyway. We have you.'

'Me?' I yelped.

'Yes,' said Jeanie. 'You swam with a selkie when you were a wee girl, you were summoned by that same selkie yourself yesterday, and you have, well… you have shown them your affinity.'

She said this with a nervous but knowing titter that didn't overwhelm the import of her statement.

I took a shaky slurp of tea-toddy, and shook my head. 'I can't sing.'

'I've heard you singing,' said Jeanie, 'over the noise of the vacuum.'

This unintentionally sounded more cosmic than she meant.

'No,' I said. 'I can sing all right, well sort of, but I can't sing them *in*. I wouldn't know what to sing.'

'Och, you mean you don't know the *song*!'

'Yes,' I said.

'Don't worry about that,' said Jeanie briskly. 'I must have half a dozen CDs with the selkie-summoning song on them. The Corries, The Proclaimers, Crannog, Capercaillie and Julie Fowlis for starters.'

'So why don't *they* summon selkies, every time they sing it?'

'As I told you, Siobhan, the song doesn't work by itself. You need to have the affinity. And besides… how do you know they *don't*?'

'What?'

'Have you ever *seen* a folk audience?'

Jeanie rang Broadford Hospital about midnight.

'Yes, miss, I know fine well I'm not a relative, thank you.' She spoke a few sentences of Gaelic, in a sharp tone. 'That's better.' She listened. 'Okay, thanks. Good night.'

'How is –?' I began.

'Concussion, cracked cervical vertebra, no spinal injury detectable. Sight, hearing, movement and speech more or less okay. Under constant observation, in a brace, but not in immediate danger and expected to recover.' Her cheek twitched. 'Yet to see how fully, but…'

I sighed and my hitherto tense shoulders slumped. 'He was lucky.'

'Or unlucky,' Jeanie pointed out. 'But yes, it could have been worse. A lot worse.'

I shuddered, imagining. 'He was brave.'

'And foolish.' She gave me an eyebrow. 'Or perhaps besotted.'

'No,' I said. 'Surely not that, he would hardly risk himself to save his rival, would he?'

Jeanie scowled at me. 'You have a lot to learn, Siobhan.'

Then my mother rang, worried after having moments earlier seen mention of a pub brawl in Kyleakin on a late night BBC Scotland headline. I had just finished reassuring her (largely by lying in her teeth, but there you go) when the Admiralty boys turned up.

'You're coming with us, Miss Ross,' one of them said.

'No, she is not,' said Jeanie. 'She is going to her bed right this minute. Come back here at eight in the morning. Bring yon officer "John" with you.'

One of them stepped out and made a phone call.

'So you'll take responsibility for her overnight, will you?'

'Yes,' said Jeanie.

He held out his iPad. 'Sign here.'

With great disdain, Jeanie squiggled a fingernail on the pad and then typed in her name, as if signing for an Amazon delivery.

'And then she'll go with us?'

'No,' said Jeanie. 'Then you'll go with us.'

The two Admiralty men shook their heads and left.

'Go where?' I said.

'You leave that to me.'

So I did.

When I came downstairs at 05:40 I found Mairi and Jeanie scoffing their usual heart-attack breakfast and scrolling their phones in the company of a middle-aged man I hadn't met before. Mairi had the look of someone who has been brought up to speed on a scandalous secret and is slightly overawed to meet its central figure. I gave her a nod.

'Good morning!' said Jeanie. Her hair was down, which I'd never seen before. 'Sleep well?'

'Not especially, sorry,' I said, reaching for a coffee mug. I glanced at the stranger. 'Ah, hello…?'

'This is Donald, my husband,' said Jeanie.

He half-rose and stretched out a hand. I shook it and mumbled something to cover my surprise. In my two weeks here it had never occurred to me that there might be a *Mr* McIntyre. I had vaguely assumed Jeanie was a widow, or separated, or something.

'Pleased to meet you,' said Donald, and resumed his breakfast.

'He's away a lot on the boats,' said Jeanie, by way of explanation.

'Oh, right!' I said.

'And it's away again I'll be going with you today,' said

Donald. He glanced down at his phone, and flicked the screen. 'Looks like you're in a wee spot of bother.'

'Am I all over the news?' I asked, dismayed.

'Only on Twitter and Facebook,' said Donald.

That was bad enough. 'What about the BBC and STV?'

'Oh, no,' said Jeanie. 'With them it's all just a wee item well down on the local news. Police were called to a disturbance.'

'People can see it's being hushed up and played down,' said Mairi, sounding well pleased with herself. 'There are three conspiracy theories already.' She rubbed her hands. 'Selkies and submarines and secrets!'

'Oh, please,' I said.

'Never you mind all that,' said Jeanie, heaping a plate of toast with eggs and bacon and black pudding and placing it in front of me. 'Get a proper breakfast in you, not that bird food of yours. Then get yourself back upstairs and put together something warm to wear on the boat.'

'The boat?'

'It's all in hand,' said Donald. 'I have waterproofs and all.'

'I have a dry-suit,' I said, a bit out of my depth.

Donald paused in his eating and nodded. 'That might come in handy, but too hot to wear until you're on the boat.'

'Well, I'll take it.'

'You do that.' He looked thoughtful. 'Do you have a mask and flippers too?'

'Yes.'

'Might be a good idea to take them and all. You never know what these creatures will want, or what form they will take.'

The previous evening caught up with me in a rush.

'Any more news of Kieran?' I asked Jeanie.

'He's asleep and seems fine,' she said.

I wanted more news than that, but her tone forbade further query. When Mairi rose at 6.15 to take the guest breakfast orders I automatically got up with her. Mairi had evidently not been expecting my help, but for a moment she looked as if she'd welcome it. Jeanie caught my shoulder and pushed me back in my seat.

'You're not working today,' she said. 'Remember?'

'But they're not here till eight!'

'Mairi will cope,' said Jeanie. 'And she'll cope without us both all day.'

The way she looked at Mairi made quite clear that this was an instruction, which Mairi took cheerfully enough. She departed, into the sounds of descending guests and clinking cutlery. Then Jeanie turned to me.

'You've got a lot to do between now and eight,' she said. 'Go up and get your warm clothes and your swimming gear packed as quick as you can, then come down to the front parlour – I'll hang a sign on the door, we'll have it to ourselves.'

'What for?'

She smiled grimly. 'Karaoke.'

This turned out to involve sitting with headphones on and listening to a Gaelic song on an old MP3 player over and over, in front of a pinned-up sheet of A2 on which Jeanie had spelled out the words phonetically, with underscores and capitals and squiggles liberally used to indicate stresses and intonation.

By the time the doorbell rang on the dot of eight I could sing along almost to Jeanie's satisfaction. Whether it would be to the selkies' satisfaction was another question. Jeanie pulled down and folded up the paper, and told me to practice the song at every opportunity over the next few hours. Then she went to answer the door.

John the naval officer and his junior sidekick were both dressed like they worked on a fishing boat. They and the two Admiralty men sat on one side of the parlour, facing me and Jeanie and Donald. They listened to Jeanie's plan, poker-faced. When she'd finished they looked at each other. There was a silent telegraphy of twitches: eyebrow raises, grimaces, nods, and shrugs.

'I suppose,' John said, 'it can't do any harm.'

And with that, we all stood up and got moving. Jeanie dashed to the kitchen to give a few last-minute instructions to Mairi, and reappeared with a woolly hat in hand, a long black quilted coat over her arm, and a carrier bag of sandwiches and thermos flasks and bottles of water which she refused my offer to carry. There was a bit of milling around in the narrow passageway among puzzled guests coming from or going to the dining room. Then out we all went, into the bright and breezy morning. There was a stutter of camera clicks, and of the corner of my eye I saw a flicker of flashes. A young man across the road hurried away.

'Papped,' said John. 'Oh well. Soon fix that.'

He barked into his phone. Not far away, a car started up.

'After you, ladies,' said John.

Jeanie and I and Donald piled into Donald's car and drove off. The two officers and the two Admiralty men followed in the black Nissan.

On the street down to the harbour several heads turned, staring for all the world as if cars were a novelty. Old Uilleam, the *bodach* I'd argued with in the pub, was striding up the road, pipe clenched, collie at his heels. He clocked me in the back seat and his eyes narrowed, tracking. I looked away as he reached inside his jacket pocket.

Donald parked down by the slipway and led us to an adjacent jetty. Just before we got there a van swerved past the end of the slipway and bumped past us. It pulled up across the end of the jetty and six young men jumped out. Their faces seemed vaguely familiar, and then I recognised them: the lads who'd glared at Cal in the Haakon's Arms.

Now they glared at us.

'Sir?' said one of the Admiralty men.

'One moment,' said John. He stepped forward. 'Gentlemen,' he said, 'do we have a problem?'

The lads glanced at each other. The one in the middle took a step to the front.

'No with you, mister,' he said. 'You go where you like. But you're no taking yon witch and the selkie's slag with you.'

Donald clenched his fists. 'Now you –' he began.

John made a back-off hand gesture behind him.

'You've been quick off the mark, I must say,' he said to the lads.

The one who'd stepped forward laughed. 'We've been waiting a while.'

'I'll bet you have,' said John. 'That's conspiracy, as well as obstruction and assault.'

'Assault? We're just standing here, mister.'

'I should point out,' John said, 'that I'm a naval officer and that these two chaps in suits are armed and authorised to use force. So I'd advise you to step out of the way and remove your vehicle.'

'Aye, right,' said the ringleader. 'Shoot us in broad daylight? No way could you hush that up.'

'You'd be surprised,' John said. 'Now move, before things turn serious.'

The lads stood their ground. I had sickening feeling that a bluff had been called. Jeanie abruptly turned to me, shoved her coat and hat in my hands, and stomped forward. She got right in the ring-leader's face.

'Now you listen to me, Ian Macdonald! Yes, and you, John

and Murdo and Calum and Neil and James! I know you, I know your parents, I know your teachers and yes, Murdo, I know your social worker. And I'll make damn sure they hear about this… this utter *disgrace*, your foul language and your insolence. Call me a witch, eh? Call a respectable young lady a slag? Who put you up to that, I wonder? Don't bother – I saw the old hypocrite a minute ago, giving me the evil eye. You should be bloody well ashamed of yourselves listening to the likes of him. Young fellows like you and all! Have you not had the benefit of a decent education? And now you talk of witches, like some illiterate *cailleach* your own great-grandmothers would have laughed at! Pitiful, that's what it is. Pitiful.'

Her forefinger, which had been jabbing forward, swept to the right. 'Be off with you before I call the police – and your mothers!'

The ring-leader had stepped back with the rest. They all looked at each other, and without a word they piled into the van as fast as they'd piled out. They reversed, turned, and drove off.

'Thank you,' said John.

Jeanie chuckled. 'My pleasure.'

She stepped back and took her hat and coat, and gave me a sudden hug.

'Don't mind what these tykes said.'

'I'm all right,' I said.

'Well!' said Donald.

He led us out along the jetty to where a most unprepossessing boat was tied up. It had a mast, a wheelhouse bristling with antennae, a foredeck stacked with lobster pots, and old car tyres and orange buoys hung around its gunwales. Painted on its bows were its registration number and the name *Pride of Dunscaith.* Everything looked hosed and swabbed, but the smell of marine life was pervasive.

John turned to the Admiralty men. 'Stay by the cars until we come back,' he said.

They walked away. 'What will these guys do all day?' I asked.

John gave me a look. 'As they're told.'

The remainder of us clambered down a few wooden steps to the deck. My knees were still shaking, but I made it. There was seating around the stern, worn blue plastic with bits of stuffing poking out. I sat down, between Jeanie and John, with my baggage between my feet.

'You're the crew for the day,' John told the junior officer.

'Yes, sir. It's been a while.'

'Mr McIntyre is the skipper,' John said loudly to us all. 'He's in charge of this boat. I'm just a passenger. The skipper is the voice of God when at sea, so do whatever he says and you can't go wrong.'

I peered around anxiously.

'Are there enough life-jackets for all of us?'

'More than enough,' said Donald. 'Under the seats, look. And there's a couple of life-rafts along the sides. The forecast's fine, so don't worry. She won't sink, and even if she does you won't drown.'

'That's good to know,' I said.

'The cold will get you first.'

John shared in Donald's guffaw. Even Jeanie smiled, albeit grimly. Donald strode to the wheelhouse and flicked switches. The junior officer cast off and hauled in the ropes, and the engine awoke with a great thudding and a haze of blue exhaust behind us. Slowly we pulled away into the channel, and then swung around and headed southwest down the Sound of Sleat. The breeze became stiffer, the waves higher. I fixed my attention on the land, as Skye on one side and Lochalsh on the other slid past. Jeanie snuggled into her coat and pulled down her hat.

'Put your headphones back on and keep singing,' she told me.

'I hope this isn't too annoying,' I said, after singing the song twice through without understanding a word.

'Don't worry,' Jeanie said in my ear. 'Not even the selkies will hear you above this racket!'

After a while, my singing threatened to get me hoarse, leave alone annoying everyone on board. I ducked into the tiny space below deck, took off my outer clothes and pulled on the dry-suit over my swimsuit, then my jacket over the top. It felt stupid to put my socks and boots back on, but no way was I walking around barefoot on this boat.

Our course turned around the Point of Sleat, the southern tip of Skye's south-western peninsula, and out to sea to the west. We saw porpoises, dolphins, and an orca. After a while the Cuillin range remained above the horizon, Canna passed behind us and smaller islands loomed, the mainland almost out of sight. The waves became higher yet, the up and down motion of the boat hypnotic. At last, about 2 pm, we approached a small island, no more than five metres high and a couple of hundred across, barely a rock with grass on top. Donald brought the boat around and within ten metres of the island's one tiny sheltered beach. The junior officer, at Donald's shouted order, dropped anchor. A gentle swaying replaced the yaw and pitch of the open sea.

The engine coughed its way down to silence, and everything else became loud: waves breaking on the beach, gulls crying overhead, the creak and clang of the rigging. Jeanie brought out sandwiches and thermoses from her carrier bag. After that late, hurried and welcome lunch, everyone looked at me.

'Well, get on with it,' said John.

Feeling acutely self-conscious, I stood up and almost fell down. Grimly recalibrating my sense of balance, hand over hand on the railing, I edged around to the bow. I took a deep breath, opened my mouth, and nothing came forth. The song had gone out of my head completely. I fumbled out and unfolded my crib-sheet, mumbled over a line or two and hummed a couple of bars.

Then I faced out to the west, across the low spit of headland and into the glimmer from the high sun, and sang.

At first it was a pod of dolphins, their dorsal fins describing black sine-waves above the swell. Then a basking shark, its size making my song skip like a scratched vinyl, swam just beneath the bows, and out again beyond the bay and out of my sight. A big black seal heaved itself onto the spit, puffing and grunting, and rolled over on its back. Others, harbour seals and grey seals, followed it on to the low rocks. Schools of porpoises arrived, leaping and twisting among the dolphins. Any doubts I might have had about what I was seeing faded: real dolphins only play with real porpoises the way a cat plays with a mouse.

I was about to sing again when John said over my shoulder: 'That's enough.'

He passed me a bottle of water. I sipped warily. My throat hurt. I coughed.

'What happens now?'

'Now it's over to me,' said John. 'Some of them must know me. We wait.'

They were all around the boat now: shoals of herring and mackerel, their silver scales and white bellies flashing; a pulsing mass of jellyfish; scores of seals and porpoises and dolphins. I fished my phone out of my shoulder bag, almost by reflex.

'Can I record this?'

'You *can*,' said John. 'Whether the pictures will still be on your phone when you've got coverage to upload them is another matter.'

I shot dozens of pictures and clips anyway as I made my way back to the stern.

'Forget photos,' Donald said as I passed the wheelhouse. 'Look at this!'

I leaned in. He pointed at instruments. 'Radar… See the five wee dots all around the island? That's naval vessels just out of visual – small fast boats, and a frigate that's in the area anyway. They're keeping an eye, all right. And the sonar? It's like we're sitting on top of the catch of my dreams.'

The sonar screen was like a pan of boiling milk. Donald swept an arm around. 'They're filling the bay and a good way beyond too. I wouldn't believe it if I hadn't seen it. Meaning no one else will believe it, either. This is a story I'll have to keep to myself or be thought a liar, even for a fisherman.'

The junior officer was up front now, conferring with John, and speaking on what I guessed was a satellite phone. I sat down beside Jeanie, who was gazing around with a rapt look close to terror.

'How many of these things are there?' she said. 'I never thought there were that many in the sea. And how did they get here in such a short time?'

'Not by swimming,' I said. 'Unless… unless they somehow knew to come here before we even set out.'

'Are you saying they have prophetic gifts?' She made it sound like heresy, which perhaps for her it was.

'No, no,' I said, 'just… predictive. Maybe as soon as things went all wrong last night, they guessed we'd soon be heading out to sea to talk with them, and they sort of did the maths.'

I was trying to do the maths in my head myself. Assuming there were selkies all around the coasts of Britain and Ireland, it wasn't adding up.

Jeanie shook her head. 'I think it's just they can get through the sea a lot faster than we know. Or than the likes of us know! John there, he didn't seem surprised at all.'

'We could be wrong about where they've come from,' I said. 'Maybe these are just the *local* selkies.'

'You could be right. It's that, or amazing speed. Either way, no wonder the Navy's worried about them.'

We stopped talking and watched the dark and bright shapes all around. That was how we caught the moment when the shapes shifted.

It happened all at once, in a second, with no transition or even a break in their motion. From sea-life to human bodies, male and female, swimming and now and then coming up for air, water drops flying from shaken hair, white teeth flashing in bold grins. Some two hundred lithe swimmers filled the bay, like a crowded swimming pool in the summer holidays. Donald gawped at them, openly agog. Jeanie herself was staring. As for me, my reaction was stronger still. My chest and my belly muscles seemed to be vibrating. The sun was baking my dry-suit. The urge to jump in and swim among the selkies had me almost on my feet and over the side. I resisted, crooking my knees hard to the seat, gripping the rail.

After a minute or two the selkies stopped swimming around. A score or so waded ashore and stood or sat on the beach; the rest bobbed in the sea, heads up like so many seals. I kept looking for Cal, but beyond a few metres I couldn't make out features in the glare. I wished I'd thought of bringing my Polaroid sunglasses.

Something was happening up at the bow. I craned sideways to look. John took off his coat and his uniform jacket, handed them to the junior officer, and then stripped naked. He was not in bad shape for his age, but the contrast with the athletic frames of the selkies was painful. He vaulted over the rail, emerged gasping, and swam then waded to the beach, up which he painfully picked his way.

John squatted down amid a huddle of selkies. They talked for ten minutes, and then John and two selkies stood up and walked to the strandline. John picked up a crooked driftwood branch, and drew lines in the gravelly sand. One of the selkies scuffed over part of the scratching. John drew more lines. The other selkie scuffed over some of them.

This back and forth went on for a few more minutes, and then the man and the two selkies stepped back and looked down and nodded. They all looked at each other, and nodded again. There was no handshake, no further ceremony. John walked back down the beach, waded into the sea and swam back to the boat. The junior officer threw him a rope, and he walked himself up the side of the boat and grabbed the rail. Donald left the wheelhouse and tossed John a towel.

He vigorously dried himself, shivering at first, and scrambled into his clothes. He raked his hair back and put his cap on and walked to where Jeanie and I sat. His knees shook. He looked down at me with what seemed like embarrassment, which I put down to his recent nakedness.

'Do you have a deal?' I asked.

'Oh yes,' he said. 'We've worked something out. The details needn't concern you, and I can't tell you anyway. It's not as formal as the Treaty, but it'll last our time, and after that – who knows? Maybe the issues in question will be irrelevant, for good or ill.'

'Great!' I said. 'So why aren't you looking pleased?'

'It's not final yet,' he said. 'The selkies want to repeat their agreement in their own language, which can only be spoken under the sea. And they need a witness to it, which can only be the person who sang them in: you.'

'Me?' I said. 'But I don't even speak selkie!'

John's worried look broke to a sour smile. 'No human does, or could. That's not the point. It's to bind them, not bind us.'

I bent over and started to unlace my boots.

Nostrils pinched, flippers on, mask and snorkel in hand, I rolled myself backwards off the seaward side of the boat into water three metres deep. The cold shocked my face. I flailed up to the surface, and trod water while I put my mask on and clenched the snorkel in my mouth. I waved and gave a thumbs-up to those on the boat, then turned and struck out for about ten metres until I spotted a boulder on the sea-bed. There I hung face down in the water, keeping myself in position above the rock with the occasional flick of the flippers or sweep of an arm. Selkies swam around and beneath me, some staring at me, others smiling.

I didn't have long to wait. The selkie I had met on the shore back-stroked beneath me, reached out a hand to the rock, and opened his mouth. From it came a song. As Cal had told me, it was more like the song of a whale than any human song – but its opening had eerie resonances and reminders of the notes and tune of the selkie-summoning song. Then it became more alien, like a dolphin's sonar, full of clicks and other sharp sounds that hurt my eardrums. I understood nothing verbally, yet I felt I saw shapes: outlines and volumes, weights and colours, currents on the move. On and on this went, with some repetitions, until it all ended on a long, graceful modulation, a yodel or a bugle call.

The selkie spread his arms wide, and looked up at me, expressionless.

I thought about what I had heard, and what had taken shape in my mind, and realised that although I couldn't put it in words or point to it on a map, I understood what had been agreed. I would know, in the right circumstances, if it were ever broken.

I spread my arms in response.

The selkie smiled, and at once darted away.

I trod water, raised and drained my mask, spat the snorkel and swallowed hard. My ears popped. I waved and gave a thumbs-up to the four on the boat.

Two or three strokes of the flippers would have seen me to the side. Just as I was about to plunge forward, a head popped out of the water in front of me.

'Cal!' I spluttered.

He trod water easily, and laid his hands on my shoulders.

'Siobhan,' he said, 'that was well done!'

'Thank you,' I said. 'What you did last night was… not so well done.'

'I had no choice,' he said.

These words weren't, as they so often are for us, as it had been for me, an excuse. They were literally true. I'm not sure how I knew that, but I did. His glamour held me like a fire in which I couldn't burn, like the heat that glows around your skin in good long sex.

'The one who did well last night was the lad who saved me. Will you thank him for me?'

'Yes,' I said. 'But you can thank him too, can't you?'

'No.'

I grabbed his shoulders. 'Will you not come back?' I cried, dismayed.

He shook his head, sending sea-water flying. 'Not to the ferry, not to my old life, not to the land for a long time to come.'

'Why ever not?'

'I've scared too many people.'

'And fascinated a lot more!'

'That, too,' he said. 'Tourists taking selfies with me on the deck? No thanks.'

I was about to try to make light of it again, to say something about phones, when I saw how grave and implacable his face was. He had no choice here either.

My eyes stung. 'So I'll never see you again?'

'I didn't say that. You have a choice. Look.'

He passed a hand downward over his eyes, and then pointed into the sea.

I pulled on the mask and hung face down in the water again.

Between me and the sea-bed was a perfect – a perfected – naked image of myself, in water within the water, like an ice sculpture or a statue of glass. She lay there, facing me, eyes closed, hair like the finest of spun glass drifting around her head, stirred by the small currents.

She opened her eyes, and looked at me, and smiled.

I recoiled, my head bursting from the water, coughing and spitting salt sea. I wrenched the mask from my head.

'What's that?' I cried.

Cal trod water a metre away from me, holding me in his regard.

'It's you,' he said. 'As you could be. As you could be forever. Your selkie self. All you have to do, to become one with her, is dive down and open your mouth, and breathe out, and breathe in.'

I stared at him, horrified. 'And drown?'

'No,' said Cal. 'Your body would become the first food of your new self. You could be with me as long as you want. You could see all we spoke of, the rise and fall of the land, the shifting of the shores, the wearing down and building of the rocks. You could take forms as wonderful and wild as those you saw here this day, and more, and learn all the life of the sea.'

I remembered the nightmare I'd woken from the day after I first saw him. That dream of being drawn down, and drowning.

And then I remembered everything else.

'I don't want to lose my life on land,' I said. 'I love you, Cal, but –'

'You don't have to lose it,' he said. 'You can go back to the boat after the change, and no one will be any the wiser.'

'Truly?'

'Truly. I swear.'

I waved to the boat again, and dived to the glassy statue's chill embrace. I placed my lips against hers, and breathed out, and breathed in the salt sea.

And then I breathed it out, and in again. The glassy statue was gone, and there was only me and all the other selkies. They pleaded with me to stay, but I refused. They couldn't stop me, and didn't try. I swam back to the surface, where Cal waited.

'Goodbye, Cal,' I said. 'See you soon.'

'You know what to sing,' he said.

'Yes,' I said.

I turned away and swam back to the boat.

'Christ,' said John, hauling me in. 'You had us worried there for a moment. Thought you'd drowned.'

'No danger of that,' I said.

The bay thrashed and foamed with leaping porpoises and dolphins. They rode the waves out, and vanished into the sea.

The engine fired up and we headed home. I went below and peeled off my dry-suit and towelled my hair, and got back into my warm clothes.

'That was quick,' said Jeanie, as I sat down.

'What?'

'Your hair,' she said.

'Most of it was under my cap,' I said.

'I mean getting it so neat,' she said.

I shrugged. We sat in silence for a while. John was poking at his phone and frowning. After a few minutes he stood up and stalked to the bow, where the reception seemed to be better.

'Have you decided yet?' Jeanie asked.

'What?' I must have looked startled.

'About your course,' Jeanie said. 'Are you still thinking of marine biology, after all this?'

'Oh yes!' I said. 'Definitely.'

'I have an old typewriter I don't use,' Jeanie said. She gave me a very odd smile. 'I think you'll be needing it.'

She was right about that, and I'm still grateful. My lecturers and tutors often complain that I'm terrible with email, and they sometimes comment unfavourably on observations that aren't well referenced in the literature, but they'll always admit that my fieldwork is exceptional, and that my essays are neatly typed.

About the Author

Ken MacLeod was born on the Isle of Lewis and lives in Gourock, where his window affords a view of seals, sea-birds, and submarines. He is the author of seventeen novels, from *The Star Fraction* (1995) to *The Corporation Wars* (2018), and many articles and short stories. He has won three BSFA awards and three Prometheus Awards, and been short-listed for the Clarke and Hugo Awards.

Ken was a Writer in Residence at the ESRC Genomics Policy and Research Forum at Edinburgh University, and Writer in Residence for the MA Creative Writing course at Edinburgh Napier University. He was Guest Selector for the SF strand at the 2017 Edinburgh International Book Festival. Recently he worked on a selection of Iain M. Banks' drawings and notes on the Culture, forthcoming from Orbit Books. He is currently writing a space opera trilogy.

Blog: http://kenmacleod.blogspot.com
Twitter: @amendlocke

NEW FROM NEWCON PRESS

Nick Wood – Water Must Fall

In 2048, climate change has brought catastrophe and water companies play god with the lives of millions. In Africa, Graham Mason struggles to save his marriage to Lizette, who is torn between loyalty to their relationship and to her people. In California, Arthur Green battles to find ways of rooting out corruption, even when his family are threatened by those he seeks to expose. As the planet continues to thirst and slowly perish, will water ever fall?

Liz Williams – Comet Weather

Practical Magic meets *The Witches of Eastwick*. A tale of four fey sisters set in contemporary London, rural Somerset, and beyond. The Fallow sisters: scattered like the four winds but now drawn back together, united in their desire to find their mother, Alys, who disappeared a year ago. They have help, of course, from the star spirits and the no-longer-living, but such advice tends to be cryptic and is hardly the most dependable of guides.

Ian Whates – Dark Angels Rising

The Dark Angels – a notorious band of brigands turned folk heroes who disbanded a decade ago – are all that stands between humanity and disaster. Reunited, Leesa, Jen and their fellow Angels must prevent a resurrected Elder – last of a long dead alien race – from reclaiming the scientific marvels of his people. Supported by a renegade military unit and the criminal zealots Saflik, the Elder is set on establishing itself as God over all humankind.

RB Kelly – Edge of Heaven

Creo Basse, a city built to house the world's dispossessed. In the dark, honeycomb districts of the lower city, Turrow searches for black-market meds for his epileptic sister when he encounters one of the many ways Creo can kill a person. A tinderbox of unrest finally ignites when a deadly plague breaks out, which the authorities claim is a terrorist weapon manufactured by extremist artificial humans hiding in the city, but is the truth darker still?

CPSIA information can be obtained
at www.ICGtesting.com
Printed in the USA
FSHW011330300821
84395FS